ZONE OF THE TENTH DEGREE

a Starscape novel

BRAD AIKEN

PADWOLF
PUBLISHING

PADWOLF PUBLISHING INC.
WWW.PADWOLF.COM

WWW.BRADAIKEN.COM

ZONE OF THE TENTH DEGREE
© 2012 BRAD AIKEN
Starscape is™ Brad Aiken

Cover Art © 2012 Roy Mauritsen

ISBN 978-1-890096-47-2
Printed in the USA
First Printing

"It's them, Jack. It's the bastards that killed Sam and my parents. You wanted to know where I've been? I've been hunting these SOB's for twenty long years, and now I've got them."

"Look, Rhoury, you've got to back off. If you fire that nuke, it could destabilize the tectonic plates and all hell could break loose."

"If I don't, these little bastards are going to keep multiplying and they're going to keep killing...more and more. I like my chances better with them out of the picture."

"Don't make me do this, Rhoury." Syzmanski signaled his first officer to ready the charges.

"Surface vessel powering weapons," the Minsky's computer announced. "Would you like to take evasive action?"

"What are you doing, man?"

"Stand down, Rhoury. I don't want to do this."

"I can't, Jack. Not now. Not after all this. I owe it to Sam."

"Sam wouldn't want this, Rhoury.

"She wouldn't want you to take me out either."

"You're not giving me much choice here, Rhoury."

"Look, man..."

"My God," Jack muttered, eyes still fixed on the viewscreen. "Something's coming up behind you, Rhoury. Check your aft viewer."
Rhoury looked. A large purple sphere was approaching from behind, dancing back and forth in the water so rapidly that any kind of weapons lock would be impossible.

"Looks like you're too late, old friend. They're gonna get me whether you launch your EM charges or not. Give Kathy my love, Jack."

"The Minsky's opening their torpedo bay," Farley said. "Should I fire, sir."

"God dammit, Rhoury." Syzmanski took a deep breath. "Fire," he said dryly.

Rhoury took one last glance at his scanner readout: no human life forms in the structure below. "This one's for you, Sam," he said as he fired the nuclear warhead toward the large sphere at the center of the colony.

The EM charges from the Lord Baltimore struck the Minsky just after the nuclear warhead launched. The tiny sub shattered just as the spherical ship approached it from behind. The shards from the Minsky's hull pierced the surface of the sphere, sending it aimlessly adrift below the Lord Baltimore.

Rhoury Callahan would not live to see the realization of his dream.

PADWOLF PUBLISHING BOOKS BY BRAD AIKEN

THE STRARSCAPE™ SERIES
THE STARSCAPE PROJECT
ZONE OF THE TENTH DEGREE

MIND FIELDS

ANTHOLOGIES

NEW BLOOD

To Laura

Acknowledgements:

For anyone who's not family or friend, you're probably wondering why you're actually reading this page; I suppose it's because you're as obsessive-compulsive as I am and you don't want to miss a word between these covers. So I'd like to acknowledge you here, on this page, for being part of the reason I like to write – to create something for people to enjoy. (I don't mind actually selling the books either, so don't feel obligated to borrow a friend's copy).

I've had a blast writing the Starscape books – far-future action-adventure stories that are a throw-back to classic science fiction, the kind meant to provide a little food for thought and a lot of entertainment. So I'd like to thank Diane Raetz for believing in my writing and picking up the Starscape series for Padwolf; Patrick Thomas, another of Padwolf's talented writers, who has devoted a lot of time to help get The Zone of the Tenth Degree into print; and Roy Mauritsen, who's inspiring artwork brings the cover to life.

The help of my writers' workshop-mates has been invaluable in picking apart every page of this book and helping me build it into what it is now. So thanks to my never-too-shy-in-their-criticism friends: Dave Dunn, Chris Negelein, David Slavin, Ben Burgis, Cliff Cunbar, Judi Castro, and our leader -- Adam-Troy Castro, who's been kind enough to take me under his wing and teach me some of the pearls that make him the incredibly gifted writer that he is.

And finally, a nod to my wife, Laura, who puts up with a house-full of writers invading our living room once a month, and who shares my love for science fiction as well as a million other things.

– June 5, 2483

The Demons of the Deep stole my life today.

I'm tired, confused, but I feel compelled to write while I'm able; it may be the only way to keep my sanity through all this.

For whoever finds this journal, my name is Samantha Callahan and my ID chip is embedded in the cover. Please tell my brother I love him.

Here's what I know so far: We left Marsh Harbour first thing this morning and headed straight out to sea. The sky was crystal clear, the waters calm. We must have been out about an hour or so when the boat lurched. What happened next, well, it all happened so quickly...the sea just opened up and swallowed us; we never had a chance. As the deck dropped away from under my feet I grabbed desperately for anything I could hold onto, but it was hopeless. The wall of water swirling around us soon became darkness.

In an instant, my world was gone.

My next memory seems more like a dream than the nightmare you would expect. I awakened to an ethereal voice telling me that everything was OK. Of course, it wasn't, but the voice was soothing and I lay still, squinting into the light. The faces overhead were serene, almost angelic; I was sure I'd died and gone to heaven.

Luxuriating in the comfort of a plush down mattress, the fog began to slowly lift from my thoughts. White silk sheets had been carefully draped over me and caressed my naked body as I began to stir.

The room was small but reeked of luxury, paneled in rich dark mahogany and furnished with the kind of antiques I'd only seen in museums; an inlaid dressing table and chair sat on a Persian rug. The tri-fold mirror that adorned the wall above the dresser reflected a surreal image of my reclining form surrounded by five angels with flowing amber gowns.

One of them smiled and told me I was aboard the Majesty, a luxury liner that now sat at the bottom of the Bermuda Triangle. She pointed to a set of clothing folded neatly on a chair across the room and told me she'd explain more at supper.

They turned to leave the room and I stopped them with a question. "My parents?"

One of them turned and shook her head.

Somehow I'd known the answer before I'd asked.

-SC

Chapter One:
Tropical Paradise

The Florida Keys
Present Day
May 27, 2503

A wistful breeze drifted across the Florida Straits, gently swaying the small dive boat anchored just off a reef at Looe Key. The sole mark of humanity on an endless expanse, the *Stargazer Two* shimmered in sunlight reflecting off tranquil clear blue waters.

It was the kind of day dreams are made of, the kind of day travel sites flash across your screen during the depths of winter while you're trapped in an apartment wondering what ever happened to global warming. It was the sensuality of a tropical paradise.

But for the two lovers who just dove into that paradise, it would have been a better day to stay aboard.

The Lower Keys had become a desolate place by the early twenty-sixth century as the effects of global warming had submerged most of the islands; what had once been a tourist-bus destination was now a remote oasis frequented only by the most adventurous divers. For a merchant space trader like TC McGee, this was the perfect place for a quiet respite, especially in the right company. And Monica Tilly was definitely the right company.

They descended to a depth of thirty feet, at which point the distractions of the reef pulled them in different directions. TC was playing with a lobster, coaxing it in and out of a small rocky crevice while Monica swam off to admire a formation of red fire-coral. He was trying to entice the lobster out into the open using a holographic lure, with little success, but the game was achieving its purpose; the silence of the deep has a way of isolating its visitors from stress, and TC was lost in the moment.

A shrill scream echoed through the communicator.

TC spun frantically. "Monica!"

There was nothing but the sound of halting gasps.

He glanced down at the scanner on his wristband where a small red blip triggered by her transponder blinked brightly against the topographical grid. She hadn't gone far.

Within seconds TC drew close enough to see her pawing at the water, trying to get away from a mass of yellow slime nearly twice her size, the features of its distorted carcass lost in the turbulence. She had gotten tangled up in the same net that had ensnared the creature, and was in a state of sheer panic.

TC's heart raced as he darted towards her. He swam up from behind and took her by the shoulders, steadying her flailing arms as she turned.

"It's OK," he said, keeping one eye on the beast. TC had seen more than his share of death; the distorted face, the contorted body, the sunken eyes opacified in their sockets…there was no mistaking it.

Monica looked right past TC and writhed in his grasp, but he held firm. "It's OK," he repeated.

After a few minutes the struggling diminished as the adrenaline rush began to subside. She slumped into his arms.

"Thanks," she said so softly the sound barely made it through the communicator.

TC held her close and stroked her back, feeling the rise and fall of labored breaths until the cadence took on a calmer pace, then he slowly pulled away.

"Now don't turn around," he said as he unsheathed his knife. "I'll have you out of this in a minute."

He cut her free, and then led her in a controlled ascent. They popped up out of the water like two bubbles bursting through the glass-like surface of the sea. A pair of seagulls swooped past and called out harshly as if scolding the divers for disturbing the serenity of the day.

TC helped Monica to the boat and made sure she had a firm grip on the ladder, then climbed aboard and pulled her up. She was trembling with exhaustion as he eased the air processor off her back; the sudden shift of weight caused her to stumble.

"Whoa, you all right?" he asked, reaching out to steady her.

"No, I'm not all right!" she snapped. "What the hell was that thing?"

TC shrugged his shoulders. "No idea," he said as he redonned his mask, "but I'm sure going to find out."

"Oh no you don't, TC McGee," she began to protest, but it was too late. He was already back in the water.

TC swam quickly, afraid the currents might have swept away his prize once the mesh had been cut. It took a few minutes to get his bearings, then he spotted it.

A pale yellow body swaying with the ebb and flow of the sea was adorned with a maze of dark green swirls that seemed to lend it a character TC hadn't appreciated at first. Its eyes faced forward, and even in their distorted state it was clear they were designed for stereoscopic vision. Many of its features were hard to make out through the netting, but there were at least eight distinct appendages: two sets of broad dorsal fins and four anterior limbs that seemed oddly out of place; thick legs with webbed feet and spindly arms with jointed elbows. The hands, designed for dexterity had three fingers and an opposing thumb; a loose sheath of skin billowed between each digit.

TC tagged the netting with a transponder, then propelled himself back toward the ship and surfaced. "Throw me a line," he yelled.

"What for?" Monica called back. "You're not seriously thinking of bringing that thing up here, are you?"

"We'll argue about it later."

She shook her head and tossed the tether line in his direction.

He grabbed it, then adjusted his regulator and ducked back under the water, following the transponder signal to its source. It didn't take long to secure the creature. He gave the line a tug to satisfy himself that he'd done an adequate job, then cut the netting loose from the rocks and pulled himself back along the tether, checking to make sure the path was clear of any sharp coral. As he emerged from the water, he waved to Monica.

"Reel it in," he motioned.

She nodded and turned to activate the motor. As it whirred into action, TC felt the line start to slip through his hand, and dropped back under to monitor its progress. Once the creature was up, he secured it to the side of the boat, and then pulled himself aboard.

Monica was waiting impatiently. "What in the hell do you think you're doing? Are you nuts? You are *not* bringing that thing on this boat! Not while I'm here."

"Now just calm down, honey," TC said, biting back a smile. "You don't really think I'm going to let this thing float away, do you?"

Monica opened her mouth to protest, but TC took her in his arms. "Ah, come on," he pleaded, gently patting her back. "You know I'd never let anything happen to you."

Her air of protest eased. "Well, I guess not, but…"

"Of course not. Look, whatever that thing is, it's dead. It's not going to hurt you now."

"Well, I suppose if it stays in the water…"

"It'll stay right there. I swear." He let go of her, and turned toward the cabin. "Got to make a call."

Monica hesitated for a second, then called after him. "But our vacation!"

It was too late. TC already had his headset on, and was tapping at the communication screen. Her plea fell on deaf ears. She threw her hands up in defeat, flopped down on one of the soft chair cushions, and stared out past the creature over the still blue waters.

*

Blake Richards was hunched over a transparent aluminum tank in his lab at the Woods Hole Center for Oceanography when the call came in.

"Hey, Blake," a young coed lab student called out, "incoming on the comm link for you."

Richards looked up, and pulled his hand out of the tank where an infant giant squid was playing. "Thanks, Leila. I'll be right there."

Blake walked into the office and sat down at the desk where the comm link was mounted.

"TC!" Blake glanced nervously in Leila's direction. "Just a sec." He got up and closed the door. "It's great to hear from you, but...," he softened his voice, "I thought we agreed you wouldn't contact me here."

Although the young lab assistant who had answered the comm hadn't recognized the caller's face, many would have. TC McGee and his long time friend Danny Stryker had attained somewhat of a folk hero status for their role in the Teconean War of 2497. Although they both now resided on the outworld of Kennedy Prime, their faces were still among the most recognizable on Earth. The last thing Blake wanted was to have someone wondering how he knew a celebrity like TC so well. If anyone started snooping into his past, they might discover that it was, to a large extent, fabricated.

"Sorry, man. But this couldn't wait. Besides, it's is about Institute business."

Blake could not help but notice that TC was on a boat. "Where are you calling from?"

"Down in the Keys. I was just doing some diving with Monica." TC panned the camera over to his girlfriend who was reclining in a chair, clad only in a skimpy, fluorescent green bikini and staring out over the placid Florida Straits.

"Not bad," Blake said, with a slight nod of his head. "So what are you wasting your time talking to me for?"

TC grinned. "Guess all that time on Earth is making you feel more human again, huh?"

Blake glanced back toward the door, then glared at TC.

"Relax," TC said. "I scrambled the signal."

"That doesn't help if someone's standing behind me, now does it?"

"Is there?" TC asked.

Blake didn't answer.

TC smiled. "I know you too well, man. You wouldn't make a mistake like that." He panned the camera back to himself. "Anyhow, as I was saying, we were just doing some diving when we came across this... Well, look, let me show you."

He panned over to the creature suspended off the side of the boat.

Blake moved closer to the screen, studying at the image. "Good God, man! What is that thing?"

"I was hoping you could tell me."

"It *is* dead, isn't it?"

"Near as I can tell."

"Good. Don't touch it. Don't move it. Does anyone else know about this?"

"Nope," TC said. "Just me and Monica. You're the first one I called, and there's not a soul in sight out here."

"Keep it that way. Upload your exact coordinates. I'll be there in under an hour."

TC nodded. "Thanks." He sent the coordinates, then disconnected.

—

There wasn't much else for TC to do but wait. He looked over at Monica, lying in the lounge chair, sunlight glistening off the beads of moisture clinging to her chest. *Ah, well. I've got an hour. I might as well enjoy it.* He pulled a bottle of chilled Pina Colada out of the refrigerator, poured two glasses and walked out on the deck.

"Care for a drink?"

Monica looked up and winked. "Hey, cabana boy, why don't you join me?" She patted the set cushion. "My boyfriend seems to have disappeared."

TC smiled. "Must be a fool."

Monica peered at TC over the top of her sunglasses. "The biggest."

"I'll make it up to you," he said sheepishly. "Promise."

Monica gazed back out over the ocean and slid her glasses up the bridge of her nose with an outstretched index finger. "So you going to sit down and hand me that drink, or what?"

TC sat down beside her and handed her a glass. "Nice day, huh?"

*

The warmth of the sun felt good against their skin, and the gentle rocking of the boat on the waves lulled TC and Monica to sleep. About an hour passed before the engines of the Wood's Hole air shuttle broke the solitude.

"Man, just when I was starting to relax." TC squinted into the sun as he watched the shuttle approach.

Monica didn't bother opening her eyes. "Just let me know when you boys are done playing."

TC looked down at her and smiled. "This won't take but a minute. We'll load this thing up, then Blake will be on his way. After that, I'm all yours."

Monica sighed and turned a bit to her side, finding a more comfortable position. "I'll be right here," she muttered to the wind.

Blake landed, pulled his craft in next to TC's and tossed him a line. The air shuttle was considerably larger than the *Stargazer Two*, but the ropes would easily secure them together, and this way Blake didn't have to worry about finding a safe zone to toss his anchor without risking damage to the fragile coral reef.

Once secured, Blake hopped over to the *Stargazer Two* and TC led him to the starboard bow, where the netted sea creature floated in the surf.

"Incredible! You really got one, didn't you?"

"You know what this thing is?"

Blake hesitated. "Well, I've never actually seen one before."

"One what?"

"I'd rather not say until I'm sure."

"Oh, come on, man."

"Hey, as soon as I can make a positive ID, you'll be the first to know."

TC shrugged his shoulders. "Stubborn android."

"Yup." Blake motioned to the creature. "Give me a hand with this thing, would you?"

"What the heck. The sooner it's out of here, the sooner I can get back to Monica."

Blake stole a peek at Monica, still dozing on the deck chair.

TC smiled and shook his head. "Let's get this thing done."

"Right. Wait here." Blake jumped back into his transport vessel, and emerged a couple of minutes later with two isolation suits. He threw one over to TC. "Can't be too careful."

TC looked at the suit. "Aw, man. I hate these things. They make me look like a geek."

"Just put it on, big guy. Nobody's taking pictures."

He leaned towards Blake and whispered. "Just don't wake Monica. She thinks I'm like James Bond or something, you know?"

Blake laughed. "Yeah, I can't believe they're still making Bond flicks."

"Flicks?" TC didn't get all the references that three hundred years of life had taught Blake.

"You know…vids."

"Ah."

"You get the head," Blake said. "I'll get…," he looked at the creature, "those things that look like legs."

The two men hoisted the net out of the water, and lifted the body over to the Wood's Hole transport vessel. The storage compartment opened at Blake's voice command and they hoisted the body in.

"Well, that's that," TC said, peeling off the suit helmet. "All packed and ready to go." He smacked the creature's arm and a stream of liquid shot out. TC turned instinctively, but not before the acid struck his right eye.

He screamed out, grabbing at his face.

"TC?" Monica called. "You OK?"

"Hell, no!" he yelled.

Blake reached for the first aid kit hanging on the wall of the storage compartment, and pulled out the eyewash. "Hold still," he said, grabbing his friend's head. He pulled TC's hand away, and winced at the sight. The cornea and sclera had already partially sloughed, and the vitreous was starting to leak from the eye. He lavaged it with the neutralizing solution as quickly as he could, then sprayed it with a topical anesthetic.

TC sighed with relief. "Much better. That stuff worked pretty quick. It must not be too bad, huh?"

Blake just shook his head. "I'm no medic, but it's not pretty. Both of you get in the air transport pronto. I need to get you to a doctor."

"But the boat," TC protested.

"I'll call the Coast Guard on the way. They'll pick it up. Get your butt in there. Now!"

Blake sealed the hatch containing the sea creature, and took off. It was a ten-minute flight to Miami's Baptist Eye Institute. Blake called ahead, and the trauma team was waiting with a stretcher when they arrived. The Wood's Hole transport vehicle landed on the roof of the Medical Arts building and Blake helped TC out. He turned to Monica, still in her bikini. "You stay with him, and ..." he reached back into a storage bin, grabbed a jogging suit and tossed it over to her. "...put this on. It'll be a little big, but I want those guys looking at TC, not at you. I've got to get back to the lab with this thing," he said, motioning to his new cargo. "Take this." He handed her a wristwatch communicator. "I'll call you as soon as I land."

She put on the suit, and got out. "Thanks, Blake."

He nodded. "Take care of him." He closed the doors and took off for Cape Cod.

*

The Baptist Eye Institute was one of the best in the world. From the surgeons to the lab techs who grew replacement tissue to the trauma team that whisked the patients from the air pad on the roof to the surgical suite, everyone knew their roles well. Within minutes, TC was transferred to an a-grav stretcher, specially designed with eye scanners linked into the hospital computers, so that the on-call surgeon could review the scans and be ready by the time TC arrived in the treatment room.

Monica was led to a small waiting area next to the trauma room, and was pacing around the coffee table when a doctor in surgical scrubs came out to look for her.

"I'm Dr. Graybill," he said, extending his hand.

Monica shook it limply.

"Are you the wife?" he asked.

She shook her head in the negative and stood silently, hugging herself.

Graybill shrugged. "Well, there's really no choice at this point anyway. All we can do is clean things up, patch the eye and let it stabilize. There's too much risk of infection for any restorative surgery now, so he can make that choice himself when the time comes."

Monica heard the surgeon, but didn't really process anything he had said. She only cared about one thing. "Is he going to be OK?" she asked.

"I don't know yet," Graybill shook his head. "The damage is pretty extensive. We've got him on antibiotics, and if we can prevent the eye from getting infected, then we can repair most of the damage, but there's no guarantee as to how much vision he'll end up with."

Monica understood, and nodded. "Thanks, doc."

"I've got to get in there," he said, and turned back to the trauma suite.

*

Monica had been in the waiting room for what seemed like hours, flipping through three month old fashion magazines until she couldn't anymore, and then futilely trying to get some much-needed sleep. She was finally starting to doze off when the beeping from her wrist phone startled her. It was Blake.

"No word yet, Blake. The doc's working on him now. All he could tell me was that …"

She was interrupted as the doctor emerged from the trauma room. Monica studied his face, looking for a clue as to how the surgery had gone, but there was nothing there. Calmly, he sat down beside her.

"Before you start," she said, "I've got a close friend of his on the phone, the one who brought him here. I'd like him to hear what you've got to say."

Graybill cleared his throat and leaned toward the phone. "Well, the damage was pretty extensive," he began, raising his voice a couple of decibels as everyone seems to do when talking to a machine. "Much of the cornea and sclera were damaged beyond repair, and he lost about twenty percent of the vitreous, the fluid inside the eye. I debrided away all the necrotic tissue, patched the eye with a synthetic cornea, and injected some Synvitrious to try to maintain the shape of the eye and allow it time to heal. I also sent a piece of the cornea to the lab, so they can begin to grow a new one for him, one that will be less likely to be rejected than a synthetic one."

Blake was listening intently. He did not understand all the medical terminology, but he thought that he got the gist of it. "So you think you'll be able to repair the damage, right?"

"Well, unfortunately, it's not that simple. In layman's terms, what I did was to cut off the dead tissue and patch up the eye. This will give it time to stabilize. If no infection sets in, then we can try to sew on a new cornea in a few weeks, but frankly, the chances of restoring his vision are not good. At best, he will see distorted images, which will be more distracting than helpful. Since the other eye is OK, he will probably just wear a patch and depend on that one. Frankly, the best alternative is to enucleate the eye – remove it. The damaged eye will always be a potential source of problems for him. The risk of infection or recurrent trauma will be high, and if he's not near an ophthalmologist, the infection could spread to his brain and kill him before he gets to help. For a guy who spends a lot of his time in space, it is risky to leave that eye in."

"When do we have to decide?" Blake asked

"No rush for now. Like I said, we've got to wait a few weeks. No need to do anything different as long as it's healing up all right."

Monica and Blake were relieved not to have to make that kind of decision for TC. They would give him time to recover and let him make the choice for himself.

But Blake was not satisfied to sit idly by. As soon as he disconnected the comm link with Monica, he placed a call to the Shakespeare Center on Kennedy Prime. Dr. Lee would know what to do. There had to be another way.

— June 6, 2483

I've been here less than a day; I'm still not sure if this is all real.

Dinner last night was bizarre. They led me into the dining hall of the Majesty, where we sat at elegantly set tables and feasted on some of the worst food I'd ever eaten.

I counted forty-three including myself. Our captors had been plucking people out of the water and skies over the Triangle for decades. Many had died by the time of my arrival; medical supplies and skills were limited.

There were four others at my table, three men of varying ages and a woman named Gina who was about ten years older than me. The eldest of the group was a man named Judd Dempster, a sixtyish gentlemanly appearing fellow with a gray beard and moustache. He's been down here about twenty-eight years. As he told me about all those who'd died since his arrival, his ghostly smile faded into despair.

Evidence and records found on board indicate the Majesty sank about five hundred years ago, but the ship is remarkably well preserved; nothing more than the wear and tear of time — peeling wallpaper corners, scuffed up furniture, that sort of thing. They have some way of controlling the environment in here to keep the ship...and us...relatively healthy. The consensus is that we're in some kind of zoo or lab. Once they set it up, they started plucking us off the surface a few at a time. The trip down is rough with all the pressure changes; only about a third survive. The rest, like mom and dad, are never seen again. Apparently the aliens don't know that we need some kind of closure. They probably just throw the bodies to the sharks.

-SC

Chapter Two:
The Shakespeare Center

The Shakespeare Center in Armstrong City was situated about half way between the spaceport and downtown. It had only been operational for six months, and parts of the complex were still under construction. The curved mirror façade of the building stretched out and around from its base, bathed in royal blue by the reflection of sapphire trees dotting the surrounding hillsides, and sparkling with the glitter of wet mist spewed high into the air from the mouth of a carved granite dolphin in the front circle. A matching slab of gray stone in front of the building was etched in bold letters:

**The Space Corps Center for
BIONIC AND ROBOTIC DEVELOPMENT**

In official circles, it was referred to as the BARD Center, but locals shunned the formal sterility of the name, and affectionately dubbed it the Shakespeare Center. The name stuck, and even the Center's director, Dr. Jennifer Lee, took pride in calling herself Shakespeare's director.

Dr. Lee was sitting in her office looking out over the valley, when her comm panel bleeped. She sighed, then spun around in her chair and tapped the screen. "Yes?"

"Sorry to disturb you, boss," her secretary answered. "It's Dr. Walsh."

Jennifer was relieved. At least it wasn't some bureaucrat determined to ruin her day. "Put him through, Sara."

The broad smile of Dr. Harmon Walsh beamed through the viewscreen.

"Looks like somebody got up on the right side of the bed today," Jennifer said.

"We got it, Jen," Walsh said. "Quigley's signed off on the human trials. Looks like you still got some pull with the old coot."

"So when can we start?" Jennifer asked. "Are you good to go?"

"Just as soon as we get the official word from the agency. It should just be a rubber stamp now that we've got Quigley's backing."

"You made my day, Harm," she smiled. "Keep me posted."

He nodded and the screen went blank as Jennifer disconnected.

Harmon Walsh was the first medical researcher Jennifer had lured to the Center. She was convinced that his groundbreaking research with primates would help her adapt a robotic eye for human use.

During her years at Omnicenter, Jennifer had perfected the design of an artificial eye for use in androids, packing millions of photon sensors onto a microchip small enough to fit into the back of an eye. Its principle was similar to a camera, in which tiny light sensors convert an image into a digital signal. Only in this case the image is sent to the android's brain rather than to a photo display. In the most simple of terms, it allows an android to see through human-appearing eyes.

This meshed perfectly with Walsh's work at the University of Maryland, where he had been working with primates, trying to restore vision after eye injuries. His team had successfully designed an interface that allowed digital video signals to be sent from a camera to the brain directly through the optic nerve, bypassing the damaged eye. The primates could then 'see' whatever the camera was pointing at.

Walsh jumped at the opportunity to join the Center. He was convinced that the camera he had been using could be replaced with the android eye designed by Jennifer, thereby allowing the injured chimps to see without any external equipment.

The work proceeded rapidly and within months, one of Dr. Walsh's injured chimps was seeing through a bionic eye.

*

Sara Jawarski had taken the executive secretary position at the Shakespeare Center shortly after the new building was completed. She had a knack for trying Jennifer's patience; sometimes Jennifer felt more like she was working for Sara than the other way around, but no one could have done the job more efficiently.

"Ooh, you just missed her." Sara said, straightening up in her chair as she looked at the handsome face of Blake Richards staring back at her from the vid link. She couldn't help but notice the urgency in his expression. "Hang on, cutie. I'll see if I can catch her."

She jumped up and ran to the doorway. "Dr. Lee…"

Jennifer, about fifty feet down the hall, stopped in mid stride. "Now what?" she muttered as she turned toward Sara.

"Ouch," said Sara. "You're giving me the look."

Jennifer raised an eyebrow.

"Yup," Sara said. "That's it."

Jennifer couldn't help but crack a smile. "What is it, Sara?"

Sara winked. "You should see the hunk on the phone who's calling for you. Looks a lot like Captain Stryker, but younger."

"Are you calling my husband a hunk?"

"You bet I am. I mean, who wouldn't? I don't know one girl around this place who wouldn't jump at the chance to…"

"All right, all right. I got it," Jennifer said. "As if I don't already have enough to worry about…"

"Ah, come on. Nobody wants to steal him…just borrow him, maybe," Sara said with a wink.

Jennifer rolled her eyes. "Just ring *the hunk* through, would you?"

Sara smiled. "You got it, boss."

Jennifer brushed past Sara's desk and into her private office, closing the door behind her. She knew from Sara's description that "the hunk" had to be Blake. No one else in all the worlds looked more like a young Danny Stryker. Jennifer knew every line of that face; she'd spent years perfecting it.

Sara smiled as she sat down and looked longingly at Blake on the vid screen. "Hang on a sec. I'll patch you through."

"Thanks," Blake answered.

Sara transferred the call through to Jennifer's private line, and muttered to herself: "Boy, some girls have all the luck." She sighed and flopped back in her chair.

*

"How the hell are you, Blake? It's been, what, six months? You must be getting pretty comfortable in your new life."

"It suits me," he said. "This link secure?"

"Tight as it gets. With the work going on around here, Omnicenter Intelligence isn't about to take any chances. Hell, even Sara can't eavesdrop on this line."

"Sara?"

"My secretary."

"Oh," Blake nodded. "That cute blonde who answered the phone?"

"God, don't let her hear you say that. She'll be draped all over you in a heartbeat."

"Doesn't sound so bad to me," Blake said.

"What? Sara?" Jennifer was incredulous.

"Yeah. Think you could introduce me? I think I'm about ready for…"

"*Not* for Sara," Jennifer said emphatically. "Believe me, that is *not* the way to get back into the dating scene, especially after three hundred years." She could see the hurt in his eyes. "Sorry, but I just think someone a little more discreet might be the way to go."

"So, what?" Blake shrugged. "You can trust her with your private files at one of the most covert research facilities in the Federation, but she's not discreet enough for me to date?"

Jennifer didn't quite know what to say to that. Maybe she just didn't think Sara was good enough for him. After all, who could be? In her eyes, Blake was the perfect man, and in a way, he was hers. "Maybe you've got a point, but Sara? I don't know. Let me sleep on it. So why'd you call, anyway? Not just for dating advice, I'm sure."

Blake filled Jennifer in on TC's accident, and on the recommendations made by the ophthalmologist at the Baptist Eye Institute.

"For God's sake," Jennifer said emphatically, "do *not* let them take that eye out under any circumstances. If I can get to him soon enough, Dr. Walsh and I might be able to implant an android eye. Human trials are just about to get underway here, and we've got a few ready to go, but if the optic nerve isn't prepared exactly the right way, the interface will never take. If they enucleate that eye before we're ready, the damage to the optic nerve will make it useless to us within a few hours."

"You really think it'll work, this android eye?"

"Works pretty good for you, doesn't it?"

"Yes, but...well, you know."

"It's the same principle," Jennifer said. "The only difference is the neural interface we had to develop to get the prosthetic eye to send impulses back to the brain through the optic nerve. We've done it dozens of times in animals."

"Animals? You mean you haven't tried it on a human yet?"

"I told you, we just got approval for human trials."

"Trials?"

"Yes. Trials. Look, what difference does it make? If I don't do this, TC will never see out of that eye again, right?"

"Well ..."

"It'll work, Blake. Trust me."

There was no one he trusted more.

*

"Monica?" Blake had dialed the number of the communicator he had given to Monica. He thought he heard her voice, but the screen was blank. "Is that you?"

"Keep your pants on, would ya?" she snapped.

Blake heard a loud 'whoosh' in the background. "Are you OK?" he asked.

"Geez, can't a girl even go to the can in private any more?"

Blake felt a blush coming on and wondered whether it showed on his face.

He heard a ripping sound, and then saw Monica holding the piece of surgical tape she had just removed from the camera lens on her watch. She flicked it away, then glared into the camera.

"There, you satisfied?" she said

Blake wasn't sure, but he thought he liked it better when he couldn't see her. "Well, you could have just deactivated the camera," he said to her.

"You didn't show me how," she said.

Blake was shocked that anyone Monica's age could conceivably *not* know how to deactivate the camera on a vid phone, but he decided to let it go. "Sorry," he said. "How's TC doing?"

"Dunno," she said. "I haven't seen the doctor since your last call, and they are keeping TC sedated. They say the more he lays still, the better."

"Well, listen, whatever happens, don't let them take his eye out. Understand?"

"Sure I understand. Just cause I've got big boobs doesn't mean I'm an idiot, you know."

"Of course," Blake said. "I'm sorry." *Boy, you don't know how sorry,* he thought. "I…I didn't mean it that way. It's just that I talked to Dr. Lee, and she said to make sure we don't let them remove that eye before she gets there."

"But how am I supposed to stop them if they say it's got to be done right away? It's not like I'm his wife or anything."

"They don't know that, now do they?"

"Yes they do. I told them when we got here, remember?"

Blake remembered. "Tell them you were just flustered. Tell them you two were on your honeymoon and you just aren't used to calling yourself Mrs. McGee yet."

"But they'll check it out, won't they? It won't be too hard to figure out that I'm lying."

"It'll be hard enough. If you're insistent, it'll delay them until Jennifer can get there."

"I don't know."

"I do," Blake said. He knew that a woman with Monica's looks could distract any man with a minimum of effort. It was fortunate that TC's surgeon was a man.

"I'll do my best," Monica said.

"I'll be back in a few hours, and Jennifer will be there tomorrow."

"Blake," Monica said as he was about to disconnect.

He looked back up at the camera.

"Thanks," she said.

Blake smiled. "Hang on. I'll be there soon."

*

Blake landed in Wood's Hole a few minutes later and unloaded his precious cargo.

"Margo!" he yelled out as he landed. "Give me a hand here, would you?"

Margo Feldman, a grad student interning at the oceanographic center, had been Blake's assistant for nearly a year now, and had won his trust. "Hey there," she smiled as he hopped out of the shuttle. "How was the big top-secret mission?"

"Can you keep a secret?"

"I don't know. What's it worth to you?" She winked at him.

Blake smiled and shook his head. "You trying to get me in trouble?"

Margo giggled. "If only," she muttered under her breath.

"Excuse me?"

"Just kidding. Of course I can keep a secret."

There was a loud *phwoosh* as Blake unsealed the cargo bay.

"Whoa!" Margo gasped as she saw the strange creature in the net. "What in God's name is..."

"No!" Blake shouted as she started to reach out towards the creature.

Margo jumped back. "What?"

"C'mon, you know better than that. Isolation precautions, remember?"

Margo smacked her forehead. "God, I feel like such an idiot."

"Forget it. I was a little overwhelmed when I saw it too."

The blush started to fade from her face. "So what is that thing, anyway?" she said.

"*Not* human," he said dryly.

"So this is what I'm learning from the master, huh? My mother would be so proud."

"Listen, I just need you to baby sit it for a while. OK? I don't want anyone to know about it until I'm back."

"Not even Gershonson?"

"Especially not Dr.Gershonson. This place will be crawling with the press."

"Gotcha."

"Look, I'll just be a couple of days. Think you can hold the fort?"

"You bet," she said with a broad grin. "Want me to run a few prelims on it while you're away?"

"No!" he snapped, then quickly softened his demeanor. "Don't touch that thing under any circumstances, got it?"

"All right, all right. Geesh, you don't have to bite my head off."

"Sorry, Margo, but a buddy of mine is lying in a hospital bed in Miami right now with a lump of jelly where his right eye used to be."

"Ooph. Sorry, boss. I didn't know."

"How could you?"

"It was *that* thing, wasn't it?" She motioned toward the creature.

"Just don't go near it, OK? Keep it tucked away nice and safe until I figure out what it is."

"Any clue?"

"I've got a pretty good hunch."

"Which…," she looked at him hopefully for a long second, "you're not gonna tell me, are you?"

"Nope," he said with finality.

Margo pouted ever so slightly, then shrugged her shoulders in defeat. "Give me a hand, boss. We'll put it into isolation tank six."

"Tank six? I thought that was shut down for repairs."

"Exactly. Engineering finished up yesterday. It's just waiting to clear inspection, which isn't scheduled for another week. The crew chief is on vacation. Nobody's gonna poke around in there until then."

Blake smiled. "Sounds like a plan."

*

The Woods Hole shuttle was the quickest transportation available. Blake didn't like to break protocol by using it for personal business, but this *was* Institute-related… sort of.

Even with the efficiency of his internal thermoregulators, Blake felt slowed down by the oppressive Miami heat. He unfastened his top button as he made his way to the waiting room at the Baptist Eye Care Institute.

"Look, Mrs. McGee," he heard a rattled voice coming from around the corner, "you've got to calm down. We're just trying to do what's best for your husband."

"Best, my ass! I'm supposed to believe that the best thing for my husband is to let you pop his eye out like some hors d'oeuvre at a zombie party?"

Monica's unmistakable voice pierced through the wall that separated the consultation room from the main waiting area. Blake looked around the room at the horrified patients sitting around listening to Monica's vivid descriptions. He bit back a smile and walked into the room.

"Maybe I can be of some help here," he offered.

The doctor breathed a sigh of relief. "Maybe *you* can talk some sense into her," he said pleadingly.

"Talk some *sense* into me!" Her voice sounded considerably more shrill on this side of the wall. Blake felt sorry for the doctor. "Who do you think you are? He is *my* husband and you are not going to strong arm me into letting you experiment on him."

The doctor looked to Blake for help.

"Doctor," Blake said. "Is Captain McGee in any imminent danger? Are there any signs of infection yet?"

"Well, no. But…"

"Good," Blake interrupted. "Then maybe we should let Mrs. McGee get a little rest and we can continue this discussion tomorrow."

"Rest? I don't need any *rest*," Monica yelled. "Let's finish this right now."

"It's OK, Monica," Blake said. "We can talk again tomorrow."

Before she could respond, the doctor quickly nodded in agreement and took off for the closest door. Blake was pretty sure it would be a different doctor on call tomorrow.

"You'd *better* run!" she shouted after him.

Blake could barely suppress his laughter.

Monica sneered. "What are you smiling at?"

"Shh," he gently motioned with the palm of his hand. "Time to cool down. The last thing we need is to be carted off by some security guard."

As the adrenaline rush began to ebb, Monica flopped into the closest chair and slumped forward, head in hands.

"You OK?" Blake asked.

"No," she shook her head, then sighed deeply, "but I will be."

Blake sat down beside her and put his arm around her shoulders without saying a word.

After a few minutes, Monica looked up. "Thanks."

Blake nodded. "Let's get you to a hotel room."

He led her out toward the lobby. They walked in silence to the medical center's hotel across the street, where they checked into two rooms. It was obvious that Monica desperately needed some sleep, and for his part Blake was thankful for a chance to defragment his memory banks, his normal maintenance cycle having been disrupted by the hectic events of the day.

*

The *Stargazer* drifted effortlessly by the rings of Roswell. Danny Stryker rarely made a trading run without TC, but this one was a piece of cake. Roswell was the closest inhabited planet to Kennedy Prime, and Danny had made this run dozens of times. He had originally planned on taking a few days off to spend with Jennifer as soon as TC had left for his vacation, but when you get a call from a guy like Hank Marshall, you don't make excuses. Marshall Vitanium was the wealthiest company on Roswell, and Hank was one of Danny's best customers. Besides, with the kind of friends that Hank Marshall had, you definitely wanted to be on his good side.

One of the benefits of the Roswell run was the close fly-by of the gaseous rings that circumscribed the planet. Danny was sure there weren't this many shades of red anywhere else in the universe. He was leaning back in his chair, hands interlocked behind his head, staring at the main view screen when the communication panel buzzed harshly, startling him out of his reverie.

"Yeah?" he snapped. "What is it?"

"*Excuse* me?" It was Jennifer, and she was apparently even more annoyed than he. "That's a nice way to greet your wife."

Danny winced, and spun around in his chair to see her annoyance burning through the viewscreen. "Uh, sorry, Jen."

"Where the heck have you been?" she asked. "I've been trying to reach you for two hours."

"Yeah. Well, the comm doesn't work too well in the rings. I just cleared them a few minutes ago."

"The rings, huh?" Her demeanor softened. Roswell held some special memories for the two of them.

"Um-hmm," Danny said, leaning back in his chair again, enjoying the last of the view as the *Stargazer* drifted away from the red planet. "Sure is a beautiful sight."

"Speaking of sight," Jennifer said, once again increasing the pace and volume of her voice, "TC's in trouble." She filled him in on the gruesome details.

"I thought Earth had the best doctors in the Federation. Can't they fix it?"

"There's not enough left to fix. But listen, if I can get to him fast enough, I might be able to get his vision back with a prosthetic eye."

"Great. TC gets to be the guinea pig, huh?"

"It's his only chance, but if I can't get to him within the next couple of days, you're going to have a copilot with a patch over his right eye. I need you back here pronto. The Stargazer's the only thing outside the fleet fast enough to get me there."

"Why waste more time waiting for me? Just commandeer a fleet vessel."

"Blake asked me to keep this on the QT. For some reason, he doesn't want the Space Corps to know about it yet."

"What's that all about?"

"Hey, I didn't have time to get into it, but Blake was pretty insistent. He must have a good reason. He said he'd fill us in when we get there."

"All right. Let me get off the comm, then, and concentrate. I'll pick you up in six hours. Those modifications you made to my engines work great."

"Of course they do." She smiled and disconnected the link.

*

It wasn't hard for Jennifer to convince Harm Walsh to join her for the trip to Earth; he was anxious to try the bionic eye in a human and TC was the perfect subject. They were waiting at the spaceport when Danny arrived on Kennedy Prime, and took off for Earth moments later.

As the *Stargazer* sped toward Earth, Dr. Harmon Walsh placed a call to the Baptist Eye Care Institute. He had briefly crossed paths before with Dr. Jack Graybill during residency, where Graybill was two years ahead of him in the program at Maryland. They had a mutual respect that Harm hoped to capitalize on, but he knew Graybill always considered him a bit cocky. After a few obligatory amenities, he explained the procedure that needed to be performed on TC to implant the prosthetic eye.

"Sounds pretty cool, Harm," Graybill said, "but there's no way on God's green Earth you're gonna get approval to do an experimental procedure here. Hell, it'll take a minor miracle just to get you privileges to do a routine case, much less something like that. I mean, you're not even licensed on Earth, are you?"

"As a matter of fact, I am. After residency I stayed on a couple of years at Maryland doing research. When I moved to K-Prime, I wasn't sure how it would work out, so I kept my license active."

"So how did it work out?" Graybill asked.

"Pretty damned good. The stuff we're doing at the Center is awesome, and K-Prime has a lot of charm once you get used to it. I sure miss watching the Orioles, though. It's just not the same sitting in front of a holovision set as it is sitting in a box at Ripkin Stadium."

"No kidding. Even in Miami, it's tough to catch the O's. I try to get out to the park whenever they play the Marlins, but it's not Ripkin."

"So," Harm said, dispensing with the informalities, "can you get me one-case privileges to operate on this guy?"

"Look, I'd love to, but they don't grant visiting surgeons privileges here very often – too much liability for the hospital. Can you imagine their response when I tell them it's to try the first prosthetic eye implant in history?"

"Come on, Jack. This McGee fellow is really important to my partner, Dr. Lee, and you know as well as I do that he doesn't stand much of a chance at regaining any useful vision without this procedure." Harm was well aware that Jack Graybill's work on human eye transplantation had ended the same way as every other medical center that had tried the procedure – an abysmal failure. "Hell, you know that better than anyone. At least talk to them for me, would you?"

"I don't know, Harm…" Dr. Graybill hesitated, obviously not too anxious to put his reputation on the line for his old junior resident.

"What's the alternative?" Harm started to sound annoyed. "It's not like *you* have anything to offer him other than a black patch."

"Now look here," Graybill fought to maintain his composure. "I resent the fact that…"

"Sorry, Jack." Harm realized that pissing this guy off was not going to accomplish anything. "I just want what's best for the patient. Hell, none of us has ever had much to offer a poor guy like this. That is precisely why I've spent the last couple of years of my life on Kennedy Prime. This is a unique opportunity. I can't take the credit for the device. That belongs to the lovely Dr. Lee over there." He pointed to Jennifer, who nodded toward the viewscreen camera. "I'm just a tool here. In fact, I could use a hand in the O.R., if you wouldn't mind."

He knew Graybill would be intrigued by the prospect of scrubbing in on a case like this; if it worked, the synthetic eye would revolutionize trauma ophthalmology.

"I'll talk to administration," Graybill said. "But don't hold your breath."

"Thanks." It was about as far as Harm figured he would get with Graybill. "I'll see you tomorrow."

*

"Didn't sound too promising, did it?" Harm asked Jennifer as his comm link with Graybill disconnected.

The side of her mouth curled up. "Wouldn't hold my breath, Harm. Guess you guys weren't soul-mates back in residency, huh?"

Harmon Walsh laughed. "Not exactly. I think his curiosity just might wear through that jealous streak, though. I'm betting he'll want in on this – first bionic eye implanted on Earth. Tough one to pass up."

"Yeah," Jen said, moving toward the comm panel, "but while you're betting, I'm going to stack the table in our favor."

She tapped the comm interface. "Computer: Connect to Omnicenter Space Corps Command, Colonel Steven Kolanski. Authorization: Lee, alpha 1824."

"Pulling out the big guns, eh, Jen?"

Jennifer smiled. She hadn't seen Ski in nearly a year. "You'd better go wake up Danny," she said to Harm. "He'll kill me if he knows I had Ski on the comm and didn't let him say hi."

Danny was resting in his quarters, tired from space-lag after the run to Roswell and the quick turnaround to Earth. Walsh went to get him just as Steven Kolanski's face came on the viewscreen.

"Well, aren't you a sight for sore eyes?" He winked as Jennifer turned toward the screen.

"Could say the same about you, you handsome devil."

"Oh, you must want something real bad. I haven't heard a line like that from a beautiful woman in ages."

"Hey!" Danny protested, stretching and fighting back a yawn as he walked up behind Jennifer. "That's my wife you're talking to."

Ski smiled. "And I meant every word of it."

Danny looked at him for a moment, then pushed at the air with both hands and plopped down in the navigator's chair. "Go ahead, she's yours."

"Hey," Jennifer protested as she turned to Danny. "I should have let you stay asleep."

"Yeah," he said, scratching his head. "You should have."

Ski laughed, shaking his head ever so slightly. "So what's up, Jen? I don't suppose this is just a social call… not that I'd mind hearing from you two a little more often."

"Afraid not. I guess you haven't heard about TC yet?"

"Heard what?"

Jennifer told him about the accident.

"God," Ski winced, "how awful."

"Yeah. Anyway, they've got him down at the Baptist Eye Care Institute in Miami. It's supposed to be the best place around, but unfortunately there's not much they can do for him."

"You've already talked to his doctor, then?"

"Well, not me; one of my associates." She motioned toward Harm, who was standing next to Danny. "He's the lead ophthalmologist on my team."

"Ah, now I see where this is leading. You want me to arrange for one of our hyperspatial med transport units to get him to your center on Kennedy Prime, right?'

"If it were only that easy," Jen winced, almost imperceptibly. "But there's not enough time. I need you to get me authorization to do the procedure in Miami. If this is going to work, it needs to be done soon, and the less we move TC around, the better."

"Now look, Jen. You know I don't have any authority over a civilian facility. Even if I wanted to…"

"You won't need to," she said. "Look, when Harm talked to the surgeon in Miami the guy practically salivated at the chance to scrub in on a procedure like this; he just doesn't have the backbone to push his administrators into making the right decision. If you place a few calls, arrange to transport TC to the Miami VA Hospital, the threat alone should be enough to push them into approving it. They'll never let a competing facility steal their thunder."

"If you really think that'll work…"

"It'll work," she said. "Heck, even if it doesn't, then we'll go through with the transfer and do it at the VA. I'd rather not move TC, but it'd be better to move him across town then half way across the galaxy."

"Consider it done," Ski said. "When will you be in Miami?"

"We're on our way now. We'll be there in a matter of hours."

"Six hours, fourteen minutes," Danny said.

"What's that?" Ski said. "Your transmission is breaking up."

The picture on the vidscreen went hazy, and the audio signal was interrupted by what sounded like static, a rapid series of random clicking noises varying in pitch and duration.

"Yeah, we're getting it here too," Danny said.

"Must be on your end," Ski said as the signal cleared. "Space Corps equipment *never* malfunctions."

Both men laughed. They'd each been victim to enough government equipment failures to last a lifetime.

"Yeah, right," Danny smirked. "I'll check mine if you check yours."

"You got a deal," Ski said. "Let me get to work on it. I'll meet you in Miami tonight."

"Right," Danny said.

As the signal disconnected, the interference resumed.

"That shouldn't be happening, should it?" Jennifer said. "I mean, once you disconnect, how can you still be getting static from transmission interference?"

"Those aren't random disruptions," Danny said, frowning and studying the comm panel. "That's an active transmission. Our comm system is recognizing it as an incoming communication, not extraneous noise. That's why we still hear it. The computer thinks we never cut off the link."

They all listened to the rhythmic series of clicks.

"Computer," Danny said. "Filter transmission and establish video link."

"Video link not available," Stargazer's feminine-sounding communications computer answered.

"Well at least clean up the audio, would you, hon?"

Jennifer rolled her eyes. "I can't believe you still talk to your ship's computer like that."

"Jealous?" Danny smiled at her.

"Maybe I should be," she said. "You spend more time with her than you do with me."

"You're one sick dude, Stryker," Harm said as he eyed Jennifer.

"Maybe I'm the one who should be jealous," Danny said. "You two have been spending an awful lot of time together at the Center."

Harm laughed. "Hell, all she ever talks about is you."

Danny smiled.

Shh!" Jennifer scolded at Harm. "That's *all* I need. As if his ego wasn't big enough already."

The comm started clicking again.

"Computer, I thought I told you to clean that up for me."

"Multivariate analysis and filtering complete. The repetition pattern of the signal is identical," the computer answered.

"Repetition pattern?"

"That is correct. Each of the three transmissions is identical."

"Computer, display acoustic spectrograph of the three transmissions on the main viewscreen."

Three lines appeared on a graph on the viewscreen, each a pattern of waves corresponding to the pitch, duration and intensity of the incoming signal. Each was identical in overall duration, and with a similar appearing wave pattern.

"Now," Danny said, "overlap the three graphs."

The computer moved the first graph over the second, superimposing the images, and then repeated the process for the third.

"I'll be damned," Danny said. All three graphs superimposed perfectly into a single wave pattern. The seemingly random interference transmissions were absolutely identical. "That ain't no solar flare," he muttered.

"Then what the heck is it?" Harm said.

"Don't have the foggiest idea," Danny said. "Computer: Check this pattern against all known transmission and speech patterns on file, and translate the communication into English."

"Processing…This communication does not correlate with any known language in my data banks."

"Can you tell where it came from?" Danny asked. "Triangulate the signal and determine the point of origination."

"Processing…Origination unknown. The exact point of origin is uncertain. It is originating from somewhere in sector beta-fourteen."

"What's all that mean?" Harm asked.

"It means," Danny answered, "that it's coming from a direction that's behind us, away from Earth, but not an area that correlates with any known Federation or Teconean planet."

"But why can't it pinpoint the origin? Shouldn't the computer be able to triangulate a source point if we're moving?"

"Sure," Danny said, "but not if *they're* moving too."

"A ship," Jennifer whispered, enlightenment grazing her face.

"Computer," Danny said, "calculate the estimated origination points of each of the three signals, assuming a uniform time between transmissions, and then determine the direction that the point of origin of these transmissions is moving relative to Earth."

"Processing…The point of origin appears to be traveling toward Earth."

"At what speed?"

"Velocity can not be determined without additional data."

The three of them stared at each other in silence.

"So what the heck does this all mean, anyway?" Harm couldn't stand the suspense.

"Oh, I don't know," Danny said. "Let's see…a message directed toward Earth in a strange transmission coming from an area with no known inhabited planets…hmm."

"Aliens," Harm whispered, wide-eyed.

Danny burst out laughing.

"You're cruel, Daniel Stryker," Jennifer scolded. "Sorry, Harm. My husband has a warped sense of humor. It's probably just some smuggler transmitting to his contact on Earth. Danny's played those kinds of games before himself; he and TC don't always transport Federation approved goods, you know."

"Hey, that was a long time ago, "Danny protested. "We're strictly by the book now."

"Damned right you are. I wouldn't be married to you if you were still taking the same stupid chances you did in the old days."

"Of course not, dear. TC and I would never take chances." He winked at Harm.

"Hey. I saw that," Jennifer said. "I'm guessing you must just think Dr. Walsh here is cute, because I *know* you wouldn't be lying to me about your trade routes."

"OK," Harm said. "I'm outta here." He walked back into the sleeping quarters and closed the door.

Danny and Jennifer watched in silence, then turned their attention back to the viewscreen, where the transmission signal was displayed.

"Any ideas on how to decipher that signal?" Jennifer asked. "I'd sure like to know what it says. Maybe it is just some smugglers with harmless contraband, but it could be Teconean spies. Maybe we should give it to Ski; let him use the Omnicenter computers to work on it."

"Yeah, maybe," Danny said, distracted.

Jennifer knew that look. "But you've got a better idea," she said.

Danny nodded. "Yup."

– June 7, 2483

Gina gave me the grand tour today. The history on this ship is amazing. From the library to the artwork and all the antiques in mint condition, it's like living in a museum. But a prison is still a prison.

We're surrounded by a giant dome that keeps out the water. I'm not sure what it's made of; we can't get close enough to touch it, but it's clear as glass.

It seems nobody knows very much about our captors, but I got to see one today. Gina took me to one spot on the Majesty where we can see them. At the foremost point on the upper deck, the dome that encapsulates my new world adjoins another dome that must serve as some sort of workshop; it's full of various ship parts and air vehicles being worked on by robotic arms. At the far side, through the clear wall I saw two of the aliens. They look kind of like octopuses, but longer, thinner and muddy yellow with dark green markings. It was tough to make out the details from that distance, but it looked like they had hands and feet at the tips of some of the tentacles.

As I strained to see into the distance, one of them looked back. It should have creeped me out, but the effect was quite the opposite, almost comforting. Gina didn't share my feelings.

They've never make any effort to communicate. I'm not sure why they're even keeping us alive.

-SC

Chapter Three:
Blake Richards

As soon as they arrived at the Miami spaceport, Danny and Jennifer went straight to Blake's hotel. He invited them up to his suite, where a freshly brewed pot of coffee was waiting. After the perfunctory greetings, he offered them each a cup, then poured some for himself, and walked across the room to a large picture window overlooking the bay.

"So," Danny said casually, "how's life back on Earth treating you?"

"It's a lonely existence," Blake said, staring wistfully out over the vast expanse of Biscayne Bay and admiring the patterns of light as the morning sun broke across its calm waters. "Knowing that I can never get too close to anyone, that I can never let anyone *really* know who I am…" He sighed, and lifted his mug in both hands.

"I had no idea," Jennifer said, walking up beside him. "We should have been to visit sooner."

"No," Blake shook his head. "If people see me hanging out with you two, they're going to wonder why a marine biologist is so tight with a couple of Space Corps officers."

"Probably so," Danny agreed.

"Still," Blake said, looking at the two of them, "it *is* good to see you again."

Jennifer smiled and took a sip of coffee.

"You did a good thing getting TC to the hospital and contacting Jen," Danny said to Blake.

He shrugged. "That's what friends are for. And you're all I've got, the three of you."

Danny looked down, rubbing the back of his neck. "Ah, come on, I'm sure you can do better than a bunch of spacers like us."

"You'd think so, wouldn't you." A smile slowly crept across Blake's face.

"So what exactly did happen to TC, anyway? I mean, you were a little vague about the details. It's not like him to take chances on a dive."

Blake took a deep breath. "I was wondering when you'd get around to that." He motioned toward the sofa. "You'd better have a seat...both of you."

Blake sat in the easy chair by the matching black leather sofa and waited for Danny and Jennifer to settle in. He put his coffee on the glass end table. "God, where do I begin..."

"At the beginning?" Danny suggested.

Jennifer jabbed him gently with her elbow and gave him a look.

"The beginning, I suppose," Blake started, "was shortly after the joining. As you know, I was stranded on the moon of Kennedy Prime for nearly three hundred years before Jennifer created this wonderful body for me." He looked up at Jennifer and smiled. "My consciousness began when the Armstrong III crash landed on the moon, and the AI 2250 computer tried to save Captain Richard Blake. Its microprocessor had been altered by the ship's rapid descent through the ion storms around K Prime, and these alterations somehow enhanced the processing power of the AI 2250 several times over. It did not have the means to save the captain, but was able to incorporate his engrams, the brain patterns of the captain, into its microprocessor. That joining of computer and man was my birth."

Jennifer furrowed her eyebrows. "We've been through all this, Blake. Don't you remember?"

He could see the concern in her eyes. "I am not malfunctioning, Jennifer. I am merely starting at the beginning, trying to help you understand my frame of mind at the time."

"Sorry," she said. "Please, go on."

"Thank you." He nodded. "You may remember that ours was the first manned ship sent to land on Kennedy Prime and I soon realized how alone I really was, isolated on the moon of an uninhabited planet. I was able to salvage the materials needed to build a communication device so I could listen to transmissions from Earth, but unfortunately there was no transmitter; my contact with humanity was strictly one way. I monitored anything I could, no matter how obscure, just to maintain my sanity. One of those things was oceanographic data transmitted by Earth's satellites to various meteorological locales."

"Sounds fascinating," Danny said. "And this is what you did for entertainment?"

"Yeah. Pretty pathetic, I admit. But after what happened with TC, I'm starting to think it may have been worthwhile."

"Ah," Danny said sarcastically, "so I suppose *now* you're going to tell us how the weather reports of the past three centuries explain TC's eye injury."

They'd done this dance before. Blake knew that Danny had little patience for his methodical explanations. He went on unfazed. "In a matter of speaking, yes. You see, amid the copious data gathered by weather satellites is a temperature-imaging map of the oceans. There is so much data collected these days that a lot of it is never analyzed, merely filed away for future reference. Since I had little else to do, I analyzed all of that data as it came in."

"Once again…fascinating," Danny said, leaning back and yawning as he stretched and cupped the back of his head in his hands.

"You wouldn't think so, would you?" Blake answered. "But one item that seemed innocuous in the beginning began to gnaw at me after the first century – an increase in thermal activity of geometric proportions that was recorded from the Zone of the Tenth Degree."

"OK. Now you've lost me completely," Danny said. "The Zone of the Tenth Degree?"

"Right," Blake said. "I've been studying this for so long I tend to forget that the aquatic thermal zones aren't familiar to everyone. Let me back-step a little."

"Oh, *please* do." Danny rolled his eyes and sighed.

Jennifer smacked his arm with the back of her hand.

"What?" he asked, innocently.

Jennifer ignored him. "Go on, Blake."

"Well, you see, by the late twentieth century, people were starting to worry about global warming. Temperatures were gradually rising, and concerns over the fragile ecosystem were mounting. Scientists attributed the effect to the depletion of the ozone layer caused by industrial pollution. There were sporadic attempts to control industrialization, but with the fragmented governments that existed at that time, it was impossible to coordinate an effective effort; many thought that the phenomenon was just a normal cyclical variation in weather, and no real threat to anyone.

"By the early twenty-first century, frustrated scientists, determined to prove once and for all that global warming was real, developed a satellite system to map and monitor surface temperatures around the globe.

"A group of researchers at the Marine Biology Institute in South Florida decided that this would be a golden opportunity for them to advance their own obscure work on deep-sea ecosystems; by modifying the new satellite system, they could gather additional data to measure temperatures on the ocean floor. An influential senator from Florida named Rees Hawley tagged a provision onto a bill the US Congress would later pass, approving funding for the project."

"Pork barrel politics, even way back then," Danny said, shaking his head.

"It was even *worse* back then," Blake answered. "Anyhow, by the middle of the twenty-first century, the new system was up and running. The data obtained was instrumental in convincing governments to pass international laws limiting industrial pollution, eventually resulting in a significant slowing of global warming."

"Ancient history, Blake," Danny said with a sigh.

"Right," Blake said, continuing. "Well, the deep-sea project was another story. A huge amount of data was needed for the ocean floor mapping, and the cost of analyzing it proved to be prohibitive. Congress was about to scrap the whole thing, but scientists scrambled to save it and came up with a compromise: the project was scaled back to look at just ten discrete oceanographic zones at various depths. The most superficial of these zones was re-ferred to as the first degree of penetration of thermal scanning, or the Zone of the First Degree. The deepest area that could be scanned was about 12,500 feet and was referred to as the Zone of the Tenth Degree. The area chosen for the latter was picked as a tribute to those who went down with the *Titanic* in 1912.

"The project was temporarily saved, but even before the first data start-ed beaming in from the satellites, Hawley died, and soon after, his adversaries cut funding for the project. All the research stations set up in South Florida were dismantled and there was nobody left to monitor the deep sea data, but the satellites kept transmitting it, just as they had been programmed to do."

Jennifer nodded. "And for a data starved AI 2250, it was fruit ripe for the picking," she said.

"Exactly," Blake said. "Sounds pretty pathetic, I know, but I was des-perate for anything I could get from home, and my circuits were firing at full speed; I was capable of processing far more data than space could send my way."

"Are we getting to the exciting part soon?" Danny asked. "Cause if we aren't, I need some coffee or something." He rubbed his eyes and stretched.

"I'll try to get to the point," Blake said.

"Fine idea," Danny added, leaning away from Jennifer, out of elbow range.

She glanced at Danny and the edges of her lips curled up ever so slight-ly.

"I expected the data to be pretty mundane," Blake continued. "What I found was anything but. You see, while surface temperatures of the oceans tend to fluctuate from weather patterns and currents, the temperatures in deeper wa-ter remain quite stable. In zones one and two, the shallowest water, there was some fluctuation, but the remainder of the zones showed remarkable stability in thermal measurements, with one glaring exception."

"The Zone of the Tenth Degree," Jennifer nodded again.

"Precisely," Blake said. "In fact, not only did the temperature *change* in this zone, but it continued to increase at a geometric rate for the next three centuries. Over the past century alone, the temperature there increased 12.8 degrees."

"Twelve-point-eight!" Jennifer said. "That kind of change could rock the whole ecosystem. It might even explain the continued global warming we've seen since the ozone layer was fixed."

"Right," Blake said, "and here's where it gets interesting. See, the center of this zone is precisely where the *Titanic* went down."

Danny shifted uneasily in his chair. "You *were* going to somehow re-late this to TC's diving injury, right? If I'm not mistaken, the *Titanic* didn't sink in the Florida Keys."

"Not even close. But I suppose you knew that," Blake said.

"Uh, yeah," Danny answered. "Not too many icebergs around the Keys."

"Right," Blake continued unperturbed. "Anyway, the most curious thing about this zone isn't that the temperature has been rising for three hundred years, it's the pattern of that rise…the unwavering geometric progression." He traced out the *pattern* with his hand. "See, over the first hundred years I monitored the readings, I recorded an increase of 3.2 degrees in the area; nothing more than random fluctuation for ocean temperatures. But in the second hundred years, it went up another 6.4 degrees."

"You said it was just in that one zone," Danny said. "It was probably just seismic activity on the ocean floor."

"Good thought, but seismic activity is episodic. The change I monitored was constant. And what's more, it has continued – as I said, another 12.8 degrees over the last hundred years. There's no way to write that much off as normal fluctuation. No way to explain it through meteorological patterns or any other naturally occurring phenomenon I could come up with. So I ran the data, looking for some kind of pattern, something that could explain what's been happening."

"And…"

"The temperature in the zone is increasing by a factor of two, once every hundred years, and if you extrapolate the pattern back, the temperature increase practically disappears by 1900; just four tenths of a degree increase between 1900 and 2000, barely more than a statistical aberration. Before the *Titanic* went down, temperatures in the Zone were stable, according to my calculations. But since it sank, a steady geometric rise."

"Which means…?" Danny asked.

"Which means it can't be explained by a single event like the sinking of the *Titanic*. There's got to be a continued alteration of the ecosystem at work, and it's changing in a pattern that's a perfect fit for a living, growing colony."

Jennifer's eyes widened. "Colony? Of what?"

"Don't know," Blake said, "but whatever it is, it's producing a tremendous amount of heat."

"A couple of degrees a century?" Danny sniped. "You call that a tremendous amount?"

"On the ocean floor? You bet. Remember, whatever is producing this heat is doing it in the midst of a frigid ocean. There's a virtually endless supply of cold water out there, so whatever heat is produced quickly dissipates in the currents. And the aquatic thermal zones were designed so that a small aberration wouldn't throw off the readings. Each zone each represents about an acre of ocean floor, so for something to produce enough heat to raise the temperature in one of these zones by a couple degrees, it would have to be huge."

Jennifer leaned forward on the edge of the sofa. "If this is a colony… What kind of aquatic life could do that?"

Blake met her gaze. "An industrialized one," he said unwaveringly.

"So," Danny said, "you think the fish are building factories from the wreckage of the *Titanic*." He turned to Jennifer. "I think you better check that bionic brain of his, Jen. There's got to be a short or something."

"Who said anything about fish?" Blake said.

"Well what else lives down there?"

"You realize," Blake started, "that you're asking that question to a marine biologist, don't you? I could bore the hell out of you with a list…"

"I bet you could," Danny interrupted.

"…but suffice it to say that none of them would have the capability to industrialize the ocean floor…at least nothing that we know of. There are still a lot of unknowns about the deep; it's extremely difficult to explore and has never generated the interest or the funding that space exploration has. My best guess, however, is that it is not any thing native to Earth that is responsible for what we see."

"What?" Danny burst out laughing. "You think it's aliens? You think Earth was invaded hundreds of years ago by aliens who wanted to live at the bottom of the Atlantic Ocean, and that TC was just attacked by one of them who happened to be vacationing in the Florida Keys this week?"

"That was my theory, yes," Blake said. "Well, not that last part, but…"

"But now you've come to your senses."

"No. Now it is fact."

Danny and Jennifer stared incredulously.

"C'mon," Danny said. You don't seriously expect me to…"

"Fact?" Jennifer interrupted. "That thing TC found?"

Blake nodded. "You should see for yourselves. TC has to remain sedated for the next two days per your protocol for the bionic eye implant, right?"

"Yeah," Jennifer said, "but…"

"Then there is nothing more you can do for him now. Come with me to Woods Hole; I'll show you."

"I don't know," Jennifer said. "I just don't feel comfortable leaving TC right now."

"Jen's right," Danny said. "Why don't you take me up there and show me this alien of yours. I'll fill her in when we get back."

Jennifer nodded her approval hesitantly. "TC's going to owe me big time."

"If I'm right," Blake said somberly, "there's going to be plenty of opportunity to see more of them." He grabbed his jacket and reached for the doorknob, then looked back at Danny. "Coming?"

*

The surgery had gone perfectly, and TC was resting quietly in his room when Jennifer arrived. Harmon Walsh was sitting by TC's bed with a big grin on his face.

"I take it everything went OK," she said.

"Like clockwork," Harm said. "You should have seen Graybill's face. He was totally lost. I mean, he had no idea what I was doing."

"And that's a good thing? I thought he was supposed to assist you."

"So did he," Harm laughed. "Hell, even if I *did* need an assistant, there's no room for an extra set of hands in a procedure like that. I just wanted him there so he could admire my work."

"Must be a guy thing," Jennifer said.

Harm just smiled.

"So when will we know?" Jennifer asked, looking at TC. "When can we wake him up and test the eye?"

"I'd give it a day or two. We don't have to keep him under as long as we did with the chimps. I mean, with them, we had to wait until the tissue was pretty much healed so they wouldn't mess with it, but with TC we should be able to let him get up and around in a day or two. I'd give it two just to be safe."

"Right. I guess I have some time before I have to recalibrate the equipment then." She would need to run a series of tests to program the bionic eye so that it would work properly with his brain once the synapses connecting the eye to his optic nerve began to fire.

Harm hopped up out of his chair. "Good. I'm starving. Let's get out of here and get something to eat."

"How 'bout we stick to the cafeteria tonight," she said. "I don't want you too far from him."

Harm looked disappointed. "Cafeteria food, huh? Oh well, at least the company's good."

Jen smiled, and led him out the door.

*

The Woods Hole shuttle wasn't as fast as the Stargazer, but it was much more practical for a short hop like the one from Miami to Cape Cod. Danny sat back in the passenger seat as Blake piloted the vehicle out of the Miami Spaceport.

"It's good to see you've made a life for yourself here," Danny said to Blake. "I know I give you a hard time, but it's all in fun. I admire you. I really do. You could have taken the easy road and stayed off-world."

"I've learned to be careful. I've found that people don't really look too hard at others if they don't have to. If you don't invade their space, they're not really all that interested in what goes on around them."

"Just the same, it's got to be tough."

"It can be trying."

"So just what have you got in that lab of yours that you want to show me?"

"The thing that injured TC."

"That's it? You got a six million gigahertz processor in that iron skull of yours and that's the best description you can give me – 'the thing?'"

"I think it's best if you see for yourself."

"All right," Danny said. "I'm game. This sounds interesting."

"You can't imagine."

"Oh, I've got a pretty good imagination."

The trip would take a couple of hours, and Danny was too restless to nap. "You mind if I call Omnicenter from your ship. Ski's been pretty worried about TC."

"Sure," Blake said. "Help yourself."

Danny activated the comm system, and accessed a secure link on the same frequency Jennifer had used to call Stephen Kolanski from the Stargazer.

"Danny, finally." Kolanski looked tired. "I've been going crazy here. How did the surgery go? Is TC going to be OK?"

"Jen said it went fine. It's too soon to know how well the eye will work, but so far, so good."

The line started to fill with waves of static.

"Man, Stryker. You'd better get that communications system of yours checked out. I'm getting the same interference I got last time you called."

"I tracked that one down," Danny said. "It was from deep space. But I'm not calling from the *Stargazer* this time, I'm on a local link. Guess your frequency's not too secure, huh?"

"Ah heck. Margaret!" Kolanski called over his shoulder.

No answer.

He looked back at the screen. "Sorry, Danny. I'd better go and find out what's going on here." He swiveled away. "Margaret, get in here and ..."

The signal disconnected.

Danny laughed. "It's good to know the top brass have their little problems too." He turned to Blake. "Say, you wouldn't happen to be able to trace the source of that interference, would you?"

"You heard it too?" Blake asked.

"The static? How could I miss it?"

"Not the static," Blake said. "The *pattern* of the static. It was rhythmic, methodical."

"I thought you might pick up on that."

"You say you heard the same thing out in space the other day?"

"Yeah, on the same frequency. Pinpointed it to a ship somewhere out towards beta-14, but couldn't make anything out of it. Figured it for some sort of smuggler's code."

"Well this one's local," Blake said. This network uses a totally different set of relays. The only thing we get off these satellites are transmissions from Earth."

"I'll be damned; must be his contact. Bold little rascal. Think you can pin down his location."

"Not a chance. Too much traffic on the local uplinks. But maybe I can work out the message; might give us something to go on. Don't suppose you've got a copy of the other transmission? The more I've got to play with, the better my chances."

"Funny you should ask." Danny pulled an audio chip out of his wallet.

"So why didn't you just give this to the geeks at the Space Corps."

"This is personal," Danny said. "Some smugglers have been horning in on a couple of my trade routes over the past few months. It's costing me a fortune, not to mention a few customers on some of the smaller outworlds. I want to catch those bastards myself."

"Tell you what," Blake said. "You fly for a while and I'll work on it. This shuttle has a pretty sophisticated computer."

"As sophisticated as the one in your head?"

"Not close, but it has an extensive communications library. It'll make it a whole lot easier to break that code."

"You've got a deal."

Danny took control of the shuttle, and Blake popped in the chip. "This might take some time," he said.

Danny put on his headset. "Computer, got any Country-Western?" He smiled as the music started to play.

*

Margo Feldman stood inside the sealed lab that held Tank Six at Woods Hole. Sundays were always quiet at the lab. It was rare for even Margo to come in on the weekend, but she just couldn't resist.

"Where *did* you come from, little one?" she asked the yellow creature floating in Tank Six. She pressed her face up against the thick glass and stared, mesmerized.

Blake had been gone since Friday night, and Margo was getting nervous. It was a sure bet that nobody would venture near Tank Six over the weekend, but come Monday morning...well, a lot can happen when people are wandering all over the place. Even a closed holding tank room wasn't entirely safe, and Margo didn't want to have to explain this to anyone.

She was deep in thought as the creature floated over. One of its hands slapped up against the glass by her face, startling the breath out of her.

"Zats!" Margo stumbled back from the tank clutching her chest. "You're not dead, are you?" The limp body floated away harmlessly.

"Of course it's dead," came a voice from behind.

Margo spun and fell back against the tank, slipping onto her bottom.

"God, Blake," she snapped, as she sat propped up against the tank and blew a wisp of black hair away from her eyes with a well aimed puff. "You scared the hell out of me." She crooked her neck and looked around him to get a better look at Danny. "And who's this?"

Danny nodded toward the creature. "It's coming back for you."

Margo whipped her head toward the tank as she scampered across the floor like a crab. The creature was motionless in the water. Danny couldn't contain his laughter.

"Very funny," she snapped.

"Sorry, sweetheart." He bit back his laughter. "Couldn't resist."

Danny put a hand on Blake's shoulder. "So which one did you bring me here to see? They're both pretty entertaining."

Margo snarled in Danny's direction.

"Yeah, but she's a lot feistier," Blake said, motioning toward Margo.

"Et tu, Blake?" She started to blush, sprawled out on the floor in her now-dirty jeans, hair hanging in front of her face. Brushing the long wavy black curls aside, she stood and studied Danny's face. Her eyebrows furrowed and she looked over at Blake, then back toward Danny. The resemblance was uncanny.

"You two brothers?"

"Nah," Danny said, lifting his hand to his mouth and coughing ever so slightly, "but people confuse us for it all the time."

Blake changed the subject quickly. "Thanks for keeping an eye on things, Margo. Why don't you go home and get some rest? I'll take it from here."

"Not on your life, Bucko."

"Bucko?"

"Uh, sorry Professor Richards, but you can't shut me out now. Not after all this." She stared pleadingly with her big, brown eyes.

Blake sighed. "All right, but take a break. Get something to eat down at the cafeteria. There are some things we need to talk about," he said, waving a finger back and forth between Danny and himself.

"But..." she started to protest, then thought better of it. She could tell by the look in Blake's eyes that he was not going to budge on this one. It killed her to not know what he was going to tell this man, but she decided she'd rather miss this conversation than be dismissed from the project all together.

"Come to think of it," she said as she stood and brushed the dirt off the back of her jeans, "I *am* kind of hungry." She walked toward the door. "Can I get you guys anything?"

"No thanks," Blake said.

"A cup of coffee would be nice, if you don't mind," Danny said.

"Sure thing," Margo said as she walked out the door. She wished it was Blake doing the asking.

*

As soon as the door snapped shut, Danny turned back to Blake. "What in the hell is that thing?" he asked, motioning toward the tank. "Where's it from?"

"I'm not sure, but I've got a theory."

"Gee, what a surprise."

"Do you remember Ariana?"

Blake had been the one to brief Danny on the Ariana disaster, the annihilation of a species not unlike humans. Their oceans had been infested with an aquatic life form, and in an effort to eradicate the infestation, the Arianans inadvertently created a toxin that destroyed all life on their planet. Images brought back to Earth by the Starscape deep space probe were gruesome.

"How could I forget?"

"Yeah. Well I'm afraid this little fellow might be the same species that invaded Ariana."

"And this is what attacked TC? Great."

"It was just an accident. The thing was already dead when TC found it. That shot of acid he took must have been some sort of defense mechanism."

"Nice. And you think these things have set up a colony in the Atlantic."

"It would explain a lot of things."

"Then what was this one doing all the way down in the Keys? And what killed it?"

"Good questions."

"Hard to believe they could survive here for centuries without us spotting them, then get so sloppy all of a sudden. You'd think they'd have retrieved the body before we could find it. Maybe they're *all* dead; some kind of plague came along and wiped them out."

Blake shook his head. "Not a chance."

"OK, I admit that would be awfully convenient, but what makes you so sure?"

Blake paused for a moment, then looked Danny in the eye. "Dead people don't send transmissions."

"Come again?"

"I broke the code."

"That static? The signal we picked up when I was talking to Ski?"

"Yes. While you were piloting the shuttle, I broke the code."

"Why the hell didn't you tell me?"

"Well, actually, I didn't break it. It's more like I broke *into* it. I was hoping to decipher the message before I told you about it."

"So what did you find out? Obviously it was enough to convince you that it was more than some sleazebag trying to smuggle viridium ore to Earth."

"It definitely was not smugglers. The code was simple, yet incredibly sophisticated."

"Oh, that makes a lot of sense," Danny smirked.

"Actually, it does. You see, it was not a code at all. It was a language, a series of clicks, much like Morse code, but varying in duration, frequency and intensity; a language that would be quite effective in a liquid environment."

"Like dolphin talk?"

"A good analogy, yes. In fact, a better analogy than Morse Code."

Danny smiled.

"Remember how long it took us to figure out the language of the dol-phins?" Blake continued. "It wasn't until the twenty-third century that we were able to understand them, and this transmission is far more complex. I don't believe it was created by humans, and certainly not by simple smugglers. No, this was almost certainly devised for underwater communication, and as far as I know, no aquatic life form on Earth is sophisticated enough to have developed something like this. I would bet it was from the same creatures that invaded Ariana centuries ago."

"The ones that wiped out every living thing on that planet," Danny muttered.

"We don't know if that was their intention. Remember, it was the panic of the Arianans that led to their own demise."

"Yeah, well it's a hell of leap in logic to assume that meant the fish-people weren't gonna kill them anyway. All we know is what's left from re-ports found on a dead world, one where life ended centuries ago. Until proven otherwise, I'm assuming these things," he pointed at the creature floating in the tank, "are here to kill *us* too."

"Let's not be alarmists, Danny. We need to study this. The last thing we want to do is start a panic that will lead us to the same fate as Ariana."

"Agreed," Danny sighed. "But I'm calling Ski. We're taking this thing to Omnicenter tonight."

"But the equipment here is much better suited to..."

"Maybe so," Danny interrupted, "but when everyone comes rolling in through these doors Monday morning, you're going to have a tough time keeping a lid on this. The fewer people who know about it, the better."

Blake had to agree.

"Speaking of which, we'd better bring your young groupie along for the ride."

"Margo? She's just a kid."

"Who loves to talk," Danny didn't have to know her all that well to figure out as much.

"What the hell," Blake said. "She'll love the adventure."

"So what did that message say, anyway?" Danny asked.

"The one we intercepted in the shuttle was from Earth. I'm still working out the algorithms to adjust for wavelength distortions that would be expected under water, but I think it was some sort of distress signal."

"Distress signal?"

"Yes. It was a repeating sequence, a series of coordinates, I believe."

"And the one from space? The one we picked up on the Stargazer?"

"Again, I'm not certain."

"Speculate."

"It was a simple message. I'm just not sure..."

"If you had to guess, what do you think it said?"

Blake looked him in the eye. "We're coming."

– August 25, 2483

Judd Demptster died today. He was the oldest amongst us, yet not old enough to die. He just clutched his chest and fell over. Probably nothing more serious than a heart attack, but we have no equipment and little medication. All we could do was hold him and comfort him. I've only know Judd about two months, but I feel like he was family. I'm sick and tired of losing family. I don't know how much more of this I can take. We left his body in a chamber by the bow of the ship. It was gone the next morning. I don't know what they did with him. Gina told me that if we watch, the aliens never come for the bodies, and we have no other way to dispose of them. We have no choice but to give them to the aliens. It sickens me.

-SC

Chapter Four:
Phoning Home

"Wow," Margo beamed, "I can't believe I'm really here."

She watched the view unfold on the shuttle's main screen as they made a low approach around the outskirts of the sculpted metal mélange that made up Omnicenter's skyline, and hovered above the spaceport landing bay waiting for final clearance.

"I mean, I've always wanted to see it, but I never thought I'd actually get the VIP tour."

The city glistened under the bright African sun. The capital of the Federation of Human Planets, Omnicenter was the base of operations for political and military leadership, and home to the Space Corps.

"Yup, this is it," Danny sniped. "The cesspool of civilization. The heart and soul of corruption, and home to every power-jockeying SOB in the Federation."

"C'mon, Danny." Blake gave Stryker a gentle jab with his elbow. "Don't kill the kid's enthusiasm."

Margo shot him a dirty look.

The ship made its final approach and docked in Landing Bay C-7, where Stephen Kolanski was standing by, ready to escort them to the lab in a secured vehicle. As special assistant to the Space Corps commander, he was one of the most influential men in the Federation. Stryker had briefed him on their situation en route.

Danny hopped out and greeted his old classmate. "How the heck are you, Ski?"

"Not bad, Ace. What's this all about? An alien? Come on, this is another one of your pranks, right?"

Danny opened the cargo bay, and pointed to the tank secured in the hold.

"God! What is that thing?" Ski asked

"Not sure, exactly."

"Where did you find it?"

"Like I said..."

"That's the bugger that attacked Captain McGee," Margo interrupted, walking up from behind.

Ski spun toward here, then turned back to Danny palms up.

Stryker shrugged his shoulders. "Just along for the ride."

"C'mon, man. This is a secure area. I didn't even let my own guys in here. Do you see anybody in here except you and me?"

"I see Margo," Danny said.

"My point exactly."

Blake hopped out of the cargo bay, landing directly in front of Kolanski. "She's my assistant."

Kolanski lurched back. "Got anybody else in there?"

Blake had donned his sensor-cloaking vest to prevent the Omnicenter scanners from detecting his android infrastructure, and slipped into the cargo bay from inside the ship. "Nope. It was pretty much just me and him," Blake waved a thumb in the alien's direction, "and he's mostly dead."

"Mostly?"

"Well, dead as a doorknob from what I can tell."

"And just who the hell are you?"

"Blake Richards." Blake thrust his hand out. "We met at Danny's wedding. I'm a marine biologist at Woods Hole. TC gave me a call when he found this thing."

Kolanski shook his hand firmly. "Richards, huh? I thought you looked familiar." He pointed at the tank. "So that's what got TC?"

Blake nodded. "Yes, sir."

"Nasty bugger."

"Sure is."

"So what do you make of it?"

"Some sort of alien life form, I think."

"Alien? From where?"

"Best guess? Somewhere in the North Atlantic."

Ski studied Blake's face, searching for the hint of a smile that wasn't there. "Last I checked, that was still Earth."

"Apparently it was just vacationing there," Margo said with a wry smile directed at Blake.

Kolanski stared briefly in her direction, then looked back at Blake. "You're pulling my leg, right Richards?"

"Well…"

Danny came up beside Blake and slapped him on the shoulder. "The doc here thinks aliens invaded Earth, attacked the *Titanic*, and settled on the bottom of the Atlantic Ocean in 1812." Danny whistled and twirled his index finger at the side of his head.

Ski looked at Blake, who was clearly annoyed.

"That your professional opinion, Richards."

"Yes, sir," Blake answered, standing at attention. "Only, it was actually 1912, not 1812, and I wouldn't have put it quite that way." He glared at Stryker, who was smiling sheepishly.

"Well, *excuse me,* Professor," Danny quipped.

"Man," Ski said, shaking his head. "It's a good thing there's nobody else around. I sure wouldn't want to have to try and explain any of this."

"So," Margo beamed, "when do we get the grand tour? I'm dying to see the base."

Ski shook his head. "And why is she here?"

He had directed his question toward Danny, but Blake answered. "She's been helping with the analysis, sir."

Ski started to respond, then just shrugged. "You three get that thing into a transport pod." He motioned to a large metallic crate by the wall. "I'll call my men to move it over to the lab."

The antigravity plinth made the job easy, and they had the alien secured for transport within minutes.

Ski looked on as Danny finished locking down the shuttle.

"Let's take this conversation inside, gentlemen," he said.

*

The trip to Kolanski's office was silent. As they entered, Kolanski walked over to his desk and buzzed the outer office. A handsome young cadet entered a few seconds later.

"Son, take Miss…" he motioned toward Margo.

"Feldman," she said.

"… Miss Feldman, here, to R&D. She's to monitor the package that was just brought in from the Spaceport."

"Hey, wait just a minute," she started to protest, then looked at Blake with pleading eyes. "Dr. Richards, don't let him banish me to some babysitting job."

"I need you there, Margo," Blake said, trying to sound convincing. "I need someone I can trust to keep an eye on that thing." It was a feeble excuse to get her out of the room, but he punctuated it with a warm smile that instantly defeated her.

"All right," she said, returning the smile.

The three men watched the door close behind her.

Danny winked at Blake. "You dog."

"What?" he asked innocently.

Kolanski cleared his throat loudly. "Shall we, gentlemen." He motioned for them to sit in the chairs across from his desk, then sat down in a large black leather swivel chair and put his hands behind his head.

"So, tell me about this theory of yours, Richards."

Blake explained what he knew about the Zone of the Tenth Degree, without revealing how he had actually obtained the data.

"I wasn't sure what was causing the rising temperature in the Zone; not until TC found that creature.”

“Ariana,” Ski muttered.

“Exactly,” Blake said.

“You know about Ariana?” Kolanski was startled.

“Uh….well,” Blake stammered.

“Yeah,” Danny interrupted. “I might have let it slip out.”

“Slip out?” Kolanski glared at him. “Look, Danny, I know you don’t exactly have the greatest reverence for Space Corps regulations, but classified data like that…”

“It seemed the most likely explanation for the transmissions.”

“Transmissions? What transmissions?”

Danny looked to Blake for help.

“You know that static you heard when Danny called from the shuttle?”

“Yeah. I checked our systems inside and out, and like I told Danny, Space Corps is clean. The interference was definitely on your end, not ours. Better check out the comm system on that shuttle of yours.”

“I did.” Blake stared intently at Kolanski.

“And?”

“And that static wasn’t static at all.”

“So what was it?”

“A distress call.”

“A distress call? From where?”

“Somewhere in the North Atlantic.”

“Those yellow things? You mean there’re more of them?”

Blake nodded. “Probably so, and a lot more on the way.”

“How do you know?”

“That interference the *Stargazer* picked up the other day? Same language pattern, different message.”

“The answer to the distress call?” Kolanski guessed.

“Best I can tell.”

Kolanski stared coldly ahead. “And how long do we have before they get here?”

“Can’t tell for sure, but judging from the three messages the *Stargazer* picked up, they are moving fast. All three transmissions were identical, probably some sort of an automated message. The time between the second and third repetition was much shorter that the time between the first two. If they were sending a repeating message, one that transmits in a fixed cycle, that could only mean that they were moving much faster than the Stargazer.”

“And she’s as fast as any ship in the Federation,” Danny said.

“Gentlemen,” Kolanski said. “We’ve got some work to do.”

– June 5, 2484

It's been one year now. I'd like to say it hardly seems that long, but in truth it feels like I've been here an eternity. My nights are restless meanderings of a mélange of memories and imaginings. It's getting hard to tell which is which; I fear I'm losing my sanity.

Still no clue how to get off this boat. I'm beginning to think I never will, unless I go the way Judd Dempster did.
-SC

Chapter Five:
The Dive

TC's recovery was progressing more quickly than anticipated and he was antsy to get out of the hospital and dig up whatever he could about that SOB that had attacked him.

"About time you two showed up," he snapped.

Danny and Blake had flown the shuttle back to Miami shortly after meeting with Kolanski, and then went straight to TC's hospital room. Jennifer was by his side, having sent Harmon Walsh off to visit with some family in nearby Tampa.

"Looking good!" Danny beamed.

TC snarled. "Jennifer tells me you flew that thing over to Omnicenter. What did they find out?"

"They're keeping it under wraps until we have a chance to figure out where it's from."

"Good. I don't want anybody stirring things up until I track those buggers down." He grabbed his jacket and headed for the door.

"Uh…eh-hmm," Jennifer said, forcing a cough through her hand.

TC looked back at her.

She pointed at TC's bottom, which was catching a draft through the skimpy hospital gown. "You may want to put some clothes on before you go dashing off to save the world."

TC looked over his shoulder, then clutched at the gown and walked over to the closet to grab his clothes. "You," he pointed at Danny. "Don't go anywhere." He turned and went into the bathroom, closing the door behind him.

Danny looked at Jennifer, who looked at Blake, and they all burst out laughing.

"Geez, what'd you do to him?" Danny asked.

"He's just in a snit," Jennifer said. "Seems Monica wanted to take him home and pamper him."

Blake raised an eyebrow. "And that's a bad thing?"

"Ah, you know TC. He's hell-bent on finding out where that creature came from, and when he told Monica, she left in a huff muttering something about him being determined to do himself in. I started to go after her, but TC stopped me, said she just needed some time to cool off. Personally, I think he was just trying to get her out of the way. Anyhow," she swept at the air, "it's none of my business."

The bathroom door flew open. "We ready?" TC said.

*

The Woods Hole shuttle made quick work of the trip to the North Atlantic and settled onto the water's surface directly over the Zone of the Tenth Degree. TC knew that Jennifer wasn't thrilled about having him make this dive so soon after surgery, but there was no stopping him; she begrudgingly acquiesced…with conditions.

"Set descent rate: 1.1 meters per second," TC said into the microphone in his dive helmet.

The protocol was the same as it would be in a standard dive suit, but unlike his wet suit computer, the VR computer only simulated the effect of releasing air from his vest.

"Descent rate 1.1 meters per second," the computer responded. "On your mark."

"Begin," TC said.

"Descent initiated."

As the marine probe dropped into the Atlantic and began its voyage, TC hung suspended from the ceiling of the VR room, in an apparatus designed to mimic the sensation of a real dive.

"Damn," he muttered.

"Pretty awesome, eh?" Blake was hanging next to him, controlling a second probe that was traveling alongside TC's.

The system was designed not only to allow divers to explore unsafe waters without risk, but could also be used for training, simulating water temperature, pressure and resistance. Anything a diver's body might have to deal with could be simulated in this chamber. The real marvel of the room, however, was the way it interacted with the dive bots.

Each dive suit was lined with thousands of sensors providing tactile feedback and instantaneous control of their assigned bot; visual input was relayed to the viewscreen inside the helmet.

Jennifer had only agreed to let TC go virtual diving under the condition that he would not allow the room to be pressurized.

"I'd love to try this place with all the bells and whistles."

"Hey, once Jen gives the go ahead, I'll book us a trip."

"Depth four hundred meters," the computer advised. "Ambient temperature, fifty-eight degrees Fahrenheit."

The two men peered silently into the darkness.

"Depth: eight hundred meters."

Tension mounted in the stillness of the deep. The descent progressed much more rapidly than any TC had previously experienced. With the pressurization system in the VR chamber deactivated, they did not have to be constrained by the time it would normally take to adjust.

"Depth: one thousand three hundred meters."

Nothing but silence and the blackness of the deep.

"Depth: two thousand meters."

They floated silently from the suspension cables, seeing only what was transmitted to their visors from below.

"Two thousand five hundred meters."

The seconds ticked by slowly.

And then Blake interrupted the silence in a near whisper. "My God."

TC strained to see through the blackness.

"It's remarkable."

"What the hell are you looking at?" TC reached up and tapped his helmet. "Damn thing must be broken. I can't see a thing."

"Adjust your spectrum," Blake said. His android eyes were far more sensitive than TC's natural eye, and the new one was not yet fully functional. "Amplify the UV by a factor of five."

TC relayed the command to his VR computer. Within a few seconds his new eye began to began to adjust and he was able to see the image on his visor: a faint violet hue glimmering on the ocean floor.

"What is it? All I can make out is a purple haze."

"Concentrate," Blake said.

TC hung motionless. "Yeah…yeah…now I see it."

The glow of light outlined a series of domes interconnected by tubes radiating from a huge central core. The main dome was at least a hundred meters across and the surrounding domes, hundreds of them, fanned out as far as the eye could see in the murkiness of the deep.

TC reached for the air bladder trigger in his dive vest, simulating the release of more air, then thrust his arms forward and pulled at the imaginary water, propelling the VR dive robot deeper.

"What's going on in there, TC?" Jennifer shouted through the intercom. "Your pulse and respirations just shot through the roof." She had been monitoring them from the adjacent VR control room, watching through a thick acrylic window as the two men dangled from their suspension lines.

There was no answer.

"TC!" she called out.

"I've got it," Blake answered.

As he maneuvered toward his friend, The VR computer projected an image of TC onto his visor; he was thirty meters below and pulling away.

"TC! Slow down, man."

But TC kept going faster, deeper.

Blake called out again… and then he saw them – three of the yellow creatures swimming towards TC, two from the left and one from the right, all out of his line of sight.

Blake released the air in his vest and thrust himself forward. The density of his android body gave him a distinct advantage as the dive bot was designed to respond to the weight and buoyancy of whoever was in the suit. He closed the distance quickly and caught TC's arm, spinning him toward the surface.

TC recoiled from the unexpected contact. "What the …" He stared wide-eyed at Blake. "You scared the crap out of me, man! I was just about to …"

"Surface! Now!" Blake yelled, as he tried to paddle upward, pulling TC along. He motioned to the left toward the oncoming creatures.

"Oh, crap!" TC yelped. He kicked frantically at the imaginary water, but it was too late. The image in his visor went black.

TC and Blake spun around aimlessly on the suspension lines, flailing in the air. The creatures had destroyed the probes, and the virtual divers had no frame of reference.

"Blake!" TC yelled. "What the hell happened?" He felt as if he'd had just been knocked silly thousands of feet below the surface.

The voice that answered was Jennifer's. "Take a deep breath, guys," she said calmly, "both of you." TC's pulse was 160 and he was breathing thirty-five times a minute. Blake's readings were steady as a rock; they were artificially generated to simulate a human, but had no real bearing on his functional health.

"You're hyperventilating, TC. Slow it down, or you're going to pass out."

The reading didn't change, and the two men continued to flail from the end of their lines like two freshly hooked fish.

"Listen to me! The robots malfunctioned, but you are OK. You are still in the VR room aboard the shuttle. Do you understand?"

TC's pulse began to slow ever so slightly, and the wild gyration of his arms and legs began to ebb.

"Do you hear me, TC?"

"Yeah," he muttered. He looked around, trying to find the source of the voice. When he spotted Jennifer on the other side of the clear wall, his respirations began to slow.

"You're on the shuttle in the VR room. Do you remember?"

"Yes," he said, as he slowly stopped waving his limbs in futility.

"Blake?" she said.

"Right, doc," he said as he stopped moving.

The two men dangled from the end of the intertwined suspension cables, their bodies limp as they swung around haphazardly, occasionally banging into each other.

Jennifer slowly broke into laughter. "God, I wish I had a holo recorder right about now. This is a picture that definitely should be shared."

"All right, all right," TC muttered. "Just get us down, would you?"

"It's a good thing we don't have to wait to depressurize," Blake said. "I feel like a complete fool."

"You should see how you *look*!" Jennifer couldn't contain herself.

The two men hung silently in the VR room for several minutes, while Jennifer untangled their cables and lowered them to the ground. They wobbled on their feet for a few seconds, regaining their land legs.

"Hang on, guys," Danny's voice came over the intercom. "We've got company."

As the engines roared to life, Blake ran over to the sensor panel in the control room and accessed the underwater viewers. Three spherical purple vessels were rapidly approaching from the city below.

"Danny," he shouted into the communications system. "Engage the air propulsion system. We'll never outrun these things on the surface. Get us airborne!"

"Right," Stryker answered, engaging the flight engines as he spoke.

The shuttle lifted slowly off the surface of the water. The engines rotated down below the belly of the ship and locked into position.

"Hold onto something!" Danny shouted as he revved to full throttle.

The shuttle bolted upward, knocking TC, Blake and Jennifer to the floor of the VR control room. On the main viewer, three spheres each considerably larger than the shuttle, erupted from the surface of the ocean sucking funnels of water a hundred meters high behind them as they raced to overtake their prey. Gaining quickly, each vessel fired an iridescent purple sheet of energy skyward, reaching out past the shuttle and arcing towards each other to form a translucent dome. Just before the apex was completed, the shuttle burst through the last remaining gap as the dome sealed behind them.

There was no further pursuit as the shuttle made its way back towards South Florida, where the *Stargazer* was docked.

"Nice flying, Ace." TC slapped Danny on the shoulder as the three passengers walked onto the bridge to join Danny for the remainder of the trip.

"Guess that kind of confirms your theory, eh Blake?" Danny said.

"And," Jennifer said, "if these little devils have set up a second colony near where you found our dead yellow friend, it just might explain that Bermuda Triangle thing too."

*

"Dr. Richards!" Margo shrieked as she saw Blake enter the commissary at Space Corps headquarters.

She was sitting at a table sipping a cup of coffee; two athletic-looking cadets were sitting across from her, something that she might have enjoyed had it not been for the fact that they were there to keep an eye on her.

"It's about time," she said. "I feel like some sort of criminal here. These goons," she motioned to the young cadets, "haven't left me alone for a second."

"We're only following orders, ma'am," one of the young men stammered. "You don't want us to get in trouble, do you?"

Margo rolled her eyes.

"Give them a break, Margo," Blake said, walking up behind the two men and putting his hands on their shoulders.

"I'll take it from here, guys," Blake said.

The two cadets stood, but did not move. "Uh, sorry, sir, but we have our orders."

"Look," Blake started.

"It's all right, gentlemen," Stryker said as he walked in. "I've got it. You're dismissed."

"Yes, sir, Captain," they said in unison, saluting. The two young men pushed their chairs in and hurried out the door.

Danny and Blake watched with amusement.

"For God's sake, Margo," Blake shook his head. "What did you do to those poor guys?"

"Hmph," she spewed, swaying her head in the direction the two cadets had just left. "Wimps."

Danny looked after them with a smile.

"Some important lab assignment, Dr. Richards. They wouldn't even let me in the room where they're keeping the creature. I'll bet they haven't even opened the containment crate yet."

"Look, Margo. This thing is getting way out of hand. I'm not sure how much longer *I'm* even going to be able to stay here working on this. We've got to get you home; it's getting much too dangerous."

"What? And miss all the fun? There is *no way* you are shipping me out of here. Not now."

"You'd rather stay here? Under guard in the cafeteria?"

"But..."

"You're going home. Today."

She acquiesced a little too easily.

*

Jennifer joined Blake, Danny and TC for the debriefing in Colonel Kolanski's office. Kolanski listened intently and watched the holo-imager in the center of the room, as it displayed the video recordings from the probes. He nearly jumped out of his seat when the creatures attacked TC's probe.

"Whoa!"

"You ain't kidding," TC said. "Scared the heck out of me."

Jennifer laughed, and the four men looked at her like she was a sadistic maniac.

"Sorry," she said, biting back the laughter, "but if you saw the way you guys looked, flailing away on the ends of those suspension cables..." She burst out laughing again.

"Yeah," TC said, clearly annoyed. "Well you wouldn't have thought it was so funny if you were on *our* end of the ropes.

"Sorry," she said again, waving her hand and looking away, trying to contain herself. "I've got it now," she said through a muted giggle, "go on."

"Right," Blake said, shaking his head. "Look, I think I'm starting to get a handle on their language. Those probes that were chasing us were sending out transmissions, presumably to each other; it gives me a little more to go on."

"Yeah, well you'd better do it in a hurry," Kolanski said. "While you four were out on your little pleasure cruise, we've been trying to reconfigure our deep space sensors to pick up that alien ship and give us a little lead time before they get here, but we don't have a clue how to track them. In fact, about all we do know about them is that their technology is light years ahead of us, and the last time they visited a planet like ours, all life on that planet ceased to exist."

– June 5, 2488

These entries are getting less frequent as my despair grows stronger, but I'll try to keep documenting salient points so that whoever may find this journal will know what has transpired here.

It's been five years to the day since my arrival. We celebrate birthdays and holidays down here to try to keep a modicum of community, but we do not celebrate arrival days any more that you would celebrate an incarceration day.

As the years have passed, life on this ship has become intolerably boring. What once seemed a massive luxury liner now seems like a small cell. I know every warped board, every crack in the ceiling. Those of us who still survive are like family to each other, but even family gets on your nerves when you're cooped up in a small space for too long. We know each other too well for surprises now and anxiously await each new unexpected arrival. It's hard to be as compassionate about their plight as we should be when they are our only source of contact from the outside world. Aside from that, my greatest entertainment is watching the aliens float next to their workroom, the motion barely perceptible. It's something that would have bored me silly five years ago.

I've watched my fellow shipmates die and new ones take their place. And as time goes by, I feel my sense of purpose slipping away. I gave up any hope of escape long ago, save one remote possibility. There are books of all kinds in the ship's library, relics of life from centuries earlier; I stumbled across one today that appears to be a detailed manual for the ship's radio. If I can get it to work, maybe I can contact the surface.

-SC

Chapter Six:
Loose Lips

When he had left Massachusetts, Blake figured this would be a quick trip – deliver the alien to Space Corps scientists, and then return to the lab. It seemed like a great opportunity for Margo, and her loyalty had earned her that much. But things had become far more complicated since then, and he was anxious to get her back to Cape Cod. He booked her on the day's last flight to Boston and escorted her to the airport. She would be home in time for dinner, and back to work at Woods Hole tomorrow morning.

"God, Dr. Richards, I can't believe you're sending me back."

"Look, Margo. You've done a damn good job, and I brought you this far because you earned it. I've never let a grad student join me on fieldwork before, at least not outside of New England. I've already stepped way over the line bringing you here without authorization. You should be thankful."

"So what more have you got to lose?" She said, gently rubbing his arm.

"Oh, no you don't. I'm not falling for that." Blake tried to ignore the warmth of her touch. "This has gotten way too dangerous. You're going home and that's final."

The boarding bracelet on her wrist buzzed softly, and then projected a neon-green holographic image above the band: 'Flight 495 to Boston, Now Boarding.'

"Come on," he said, picking up the pace. "I don't intend to let you miss this one."

He accompanied her as far as the jetway. "Give me a call when you get there."

She glared at him, then spun on her heels and walked away without saying a word.

"Ouch," he muttered softly, then shrugged and turned away.

He was anxious to get back to Space Corps Headquarters. A lot of progress had been made on the language algorithms of the aliens – Silesians, they'd called themselves in the message – but he needed to learn a lot more before he attempted to make contact.

*

Margo peered out the window from her seat aboard flight 495. It was hard to make out, but she was pretty sure it was Dr. Richards she saw scurrying away from the gate.

"Ladies and gentlemen, please take your seats so we can prepare for take-off."

"Wait!" Margo yelled as she jumped out of her seat and ran toward the front of the plane. "I forgot my bag." She brushed past the stewardess in the aisle.

"Ma'am, please take your seat. There's no time. And besides, if you left a bag unattended, it can't come on the plane now."

"Then I won't get back on. I need that bag," she snapped as she grabbed the arm of the second attendant, who was reaching to close the door, and pushed him out of the way."

"Hey!"

"Sorry," Margo yelled as she jumped through the door and ran into the boarding tunnel towards the gate. She didn't need to look back to know the door was sealing shut behind her.

As she ran through the terminal, she pulled out her phone and dialed. "Kenny?"

"Who is this?" the voice on the other end of the line said. I can't see a damned thing. Is your phone working OK?"

"Zats, Kenny!" Margo stopped for a second and held the phone up to her face. "You happy now? Didn't you recognize my voice?"

Though Kenny had never told her, Margo knew he had a major crush on her, a fact that she'd used to her advantage on more than one occasion.

"I just wasn't sure, that's all. What're you running for, anyway? Everything OK? You and Richards have been gone an awfully long time. The rumors are starting to fly."

Jealousy hung on his voice like maple syrup, much to Margo's satisfaction.

"You want to know what this is all about?" she asked.

"Damned right I do."

"Then shut up and listen carefully."

Margo told him about the creature in the Keys, and the even more amazing discovery of the alien colony in the North Atlantic.

"I know it's all pretty tough to swallow, but it's true, every word of it. I'm going to stick around and try to get back into the Space Corps Center; I've got to know what's going on in there. What I need from you is to get word to my folks that I'm OK, and tell them at the lab that you picked me up at Logan and took me home. Tell them I caught a horrendous cold on the trip and I'm home in bed, taking a few days off to recover." She smiled playfully. "Can you do that for me, Kenny?"

"Sure," he said sheepishly.

"Good boy. Gotta go."

"But…"

Margo closed the phone and tossed it back into her purse.

*

"Hey, Rhoury," Kenny said, as he stared at the wild-eyed disheveled man on the video screen in his apartment. "You're not going to believe what I just heard."

Rhoury Callahan was, by any definition, a rebel. His obsession with the Bermuda Triangle earned him a psychological discharge from the Navy, and gave him the opportunity to pursue those interests in earnest. He knew naval protocol well enough to make sure the authorities never got in his way when he needed to poke around restricted areas, and his research eventually convinced him there was really only one explanation for all of the ships and planes that had vanished: some sort of intelligent life had colonized the ocean floor in the Bermuda Triangle.

Rhoury learned early on that his quest would take a great deal of money, and founded the New Ocean Society, an organization dedicated to exposing the truth about what had invaded the oceans. His Internet site garnered thousands of supporters of all ages. Some were teenagers, easily influenced by the charismatic Callahan, but many were well established citizens who had lost loved ones in the Bermuda Triangle, and who were equally convinced that there was some evil force at work in the abyss.

Contributions mounted quickly, and funded his earliest explorations into the Triangle. Much to his disappointment, Rhoury's first trips yielded only the discovery of sunken ships, some of which were filled with long-lost riches. It was not what he had hoped to find, but the money served to expand his capabilities. The most recent acquisition of the New Ocean Society was a discarded nuclear submarine with one remaining warhead. Black marketers had traded the nuke for centuries, a long lost relic of Tehran's underground nuclear program in the early twenty-first century that had nearly started World War Three. Rhoury hoped it would still work if he ever found the bastards who had invaded the Triangle.

"Totally warped, man," Rhoury muttered after hearing the story that Margo had relayed to Kenny. "I knew it. I knew those bastards were here, only I never thought to look that far north. Pretty clever, huh? They hid in the North Atlantic, and did all their dirty work in the Triangle."

It didn't really make much sense to Kenny, but who was he to disagree? He had latched on to the New Ocean Society a couple of years back, a product of a gawky teen-aged boy's long hours on the Internet. He'd have rather been with girls, especially ones like Margo Feldman, but that had never been an option for him. Rhoury Callahan made him feel like he was part of something important; Kenny revered the man.

"They probably have a second colony in the Triangle, but at least we know where to start. It's at the *Titanic* crash site, huh?"

"Yup," Kenny said proudly. 41°43'57" N by 49°56'49" W

"No shit, Sherlock," Rhoury said.

Kenny's smile faded as a grin crept across Rhoury's face. "And I know just what to do about it."

"The nuke?" Kenny asked.

"Good work, dude." Rhoury said.

The line went dead.

"God, what have I done?" Kenny muttered.

– June 17, 2493

I finally got the radio to work!

Even though everyone thought I was nuts, they all pitched in scouring the ship for parts. Every once in a while, the aliens would even send some random electronics our way; just toys most of the time. They were too smart to send anything that could be used as a weapon or communicator, but anything they sent our way brought new hope.

Turns out Jeremy Grissom is an electrical engineer. He was an immense help in deciphering some of the blueprints and fabricating replacement parts. The toughest part was battery power; toys don't often utilize antimatter cells and this thing takes a lot of juice to get it working. But today we got lucky. I don't know if this one just slipped by or if the aliens wanted to see what we'd do with it; I don't really care. Manna from heaven.

I was never so happy to hear static, even if it was simply dead air.

-SC

– Sept 12, 2493

Still no reply to my hails. I'm not sure why I'm boring you with more frequent entries again other than to vent my enthusiasm. Everyone was very excited when I told them about the radio, but after weeks of listening to static, the interest has waned. It's just me in that room for hours each day now.

I've been trying for two months to contact the surface without a hint of a response. I don't know if my signals are getting out, but I doubt it. The dome must be shielding them. Nothing's getting in, that's for sure. I suspect the dome shields against any scans from the surface as well. If anybody is looking for us, they'll never find us.

I'm going to try to establish contact with our captors. Not too optimistic.

-SC

Chapter Seven:
Oops

Margo sat in the main lobby of the Space Corps Center trying to make herself obscure, and observed the passers by. The guards were chatting away, more concerned with their conversation than their surroundings. By all appearances, they were merely window dressing.

An elderly man entered the building, and as he passed by Margo, he smiled and gave her a wink. She couldn't quite place him, but he looked so...

"Ten-hut!" one of the guards shouted. "President on deck." They all snapped to attention and saluted.

Margo smacked the palm of her hand against her forehead as she bolted upright, straining to get a closer look. "God, I'm such an idiot!" she muttered. She couldn't believe she hadn't recognized the President of Earth. He had smiled at her, *winked* at her, for God's sake, and she had just yawned and turned away. How embarrassing. He looked so different in real life; smaller somehow.

As she walked toward the security screening system to get a closer look, she smacked right into an iron bar of an arm.

"Please stay where you are until the president has entered the elevator, ma'am."

Three secret service agents had come in behind President Atkinson, and were following him through the scanners.

"Swanson. Clearance code gamma 694," the first one said.

The system analyzed his voice pattern and scanned his retinas as he entered, while the ID chip embedded in his sidearm was checked against the Space Corps database. Before he had crossed the threshold, the computer had verified his identity, security clearance level and sidearm registration. If they hadn't matched, the lobby would have locked down, and he would have been stunned out of consciousness. The Space Corps guards were merely a redundant back-up system.

Margo watched them pass. "Like I've got a chance in hell of getting in there," she muttered.

The guards went back to their idle chatter after the president's entourage had entered the elevator. One of them smiled at Margo, who was inadvertently staring in his direction, plotting her next move. She plopped back down on the padded bench, dejected.

As she sat, staring at the ceiling, her phone rang, disturbing the security guards' discussion about Sunday's upcoming game.

"Sorry," she said in their direction.

Margo glanced at the phone and saw Kenny fidgeting nervously, waiting for her to answer. She flipped it open.

"Kenny? Everything OK?"

"Uh...I think I screwed up."

"What!" she snapped.

The three guards looked up and admonished her in silence.

"Sorry, guys," she said, waving them off and turning to take her conversation outside. She strolled toward a large oak tree in a field of grass adorning the grounds in front of the building, far from the ears of any would-be eavesdroppers.

"You screwed up?" she said into the phone. "Define 'screwed up.' You better not have gotten me fired."

"No, no, nothing like that," Kenny said.

She sighed in relief. "It's a good thing. Because if..."

"Much worse," he interrupted.

Margo paused ever so briefly. "Worse? What'd you do, Kenny?" Her eyes narrowed.

"I kind of told Rhoury about your discovery."

"Rhoury? Who the hell is Rhoury?"

"Rhoury Callahan. You know, that guy I told you about. The one who runs the New Ocean Society."

"That fruitcake? Are you nuts?"

"No," Kenny looked hurt, "but I think he is. I think he's gonna nuke 'em."

"He's gonna what!"

"Like I said," Kenny said sheepishly. "I screwed up, didn't I?"

"Big time, Kenny. Big time."

Margo hung up, sat down against a tree and buried her head in her hands. "This is not happening. This is not happening," she kept repeating.

"What's not happening, sweetie?" One of the grounds guards walked up beside her, a kindly appearing gentleman with short-cropped gray hair protruding from around his green cap. "You in some kind of trouble?"

Margo looked up. "You don't know the half of it."

"Here," he said, offering her his hand. "Let's start by getting you up off that damp ground.

She took his hand and stood. "Thanks."

"My pleasure, miss. Now, what seems to be the trouble? You need a ride home or something?"

"Oh, just some bad news. I'll be OK." She brushed herself off.

The guard looked dubious.

"Really," she said with a smile. "I'll just go inside and make a call. My friend works in there," she pointed to the Space Corps building. "He'll give me a lift home."

"You sure now?"

"I'm sure," she blinked with a smile. "Thank you so much for your kindness. I feel much better now."

"Well, if you're sure, then," he said.

She nodded and walked back inside. The three guards by the security scanner glanced over briefly, then went back to their pre-game predictions.

Margo reluctantly picked up her phone. "Call Blake Richards," she said to it.

"Margo?" Blake answered. "Everything OK?" He looked behind her on the small video screen on his phone. "That doesn't look like a plane...where are you?"

"Uh, yeah. About that."

"Margo?" he sounded annoyed.

"I kind of messed up, Dr. Richards."

"You got off the plane, didn't you?"

"Yup. Mea culpa."

"Look, Margo. I don't have time for this. I can't believe you didn't go back to Boston like we agreed."

"Who agreed?"

"Margo…?" The frustration in his voice was palpable.

"Yeah, well, that's not the bad news," she said.

"I don't think I want to hear this. Do I want to hear this?"

"Probably not."

"But you're going to tell me anyway, aren't you?"

"I think I'd better. If you call the front entrance and get me clearance, I'll come up and explain."

"*What?* You're at Space Corps?"

"Not too close to Boston, huh?"

"Margo..."

"No need to send an escort," she said with a meek smile. "I know my way. Just get me clearance."

The line disconnected, and a few seconds later the guards' phone rang.

"Yes, sir. Right away, sir."

One of the guards stood up and motioned toward Margo. "You Feldman?" he asked.

Margo nodded.

"This way, ma'am. Private Henry here will take you to the colonel's office." He pointed to one of the other men.

Margo passed through security and started to walk past the guards. "Oh, that's OK. I know my way."

The head guard grabbed her arm, stopping her in her tracks. He was considerably stronger than he looked.

"I said," he glared at her, "Private Henry here will escort you."

"Actually, you said: Private Henry here will take you to the colonel's office," she said in a husky voice mimicking the guard.

He was not amused. He motioned to Henry, who escorted Margo away.

*

"Come," Kolanski said, as he heard a knock on the door. Blake Richards was already there updating Kolanski on his progress.

"Sorry to disturb you, Colonel," the private said, pulling Margo into the room gently.

She yanked her arm away. "Thank you," she said curtly.

Private Henry looked pleadingly toward Kolanski.

"Dismissed," Kolanski said.

Henry turned and walked away as quickly as his feet could carry him.

Blake laughed. "She has that effect on people."

"Sit," Kolanski said to her.

Margo took a seat.

"All right, Margo." Blake said. "Let's have it."

"Look, I'm no traitor," she said nervously. "I love the Federation and the Corps as much as anybody."

Kolanski shifted uneasily. "I don't think I like the way this story is starting, young lady."

"Well, just wait. It gets much worse." Her attempt at a smile was woeful, and the blank stares she met across the table didn't make things any easier. "See, I just wanted in on the action. I mean, I wasn't about to be sitting on some plane heading for Logan and miss out on the most exciting thing to ever happen to this planet."

"Let's hope it's not that exciting," Ski said.

Margo looked at him with a *Why on Earth not?* kind of look, then directed the conversation to Blake. "If I was going to stay here, I needed to get somebody to cover for me at work, so I called Kenny and told him what was going on."

"You told Kenny? Weird Kenny?"

Margo laughed. "Geez, I didn't know the profs called him that too."

"Yeah, well, let's just keep that between you and me, huh? So just what exactly did you tell him?"

"Everything," she said very matter-of-factly. "I couldn't very well expect him to lie for me without a good reason, now could I?"

Blake shook his head. "Kenny, huh? Well, I guess it could be worse."

"Oh, trust me," Margo said. "It certainly could be."

The two men looked at her apprehensively.

"See, it turns out Kenny's in this thing called the New Ocean Society, and he kind of mentioned the colony to its leader, a guy named Rhoury Callahan."

"Callahan!" Blake shrieked. "That nut case? What the hell did he tell him for? No, wait. Let me guess. He thinks our little yellow guy is one of the aliens Callahan's been hunting."

"Uh-huh," she nodded with grimace and told them what she knew of Callahan's plans. "Please don't kill me."

Before Kolanski could respond, his communication screen sounded.

"What is it?" he snapped.

"Sorry to disturb you, sir," said the young airman on the screen, "but you asked to be notified immediately if there were any aberrations on our deep space scans."

"Yes."

"Well, it seems we've picked something up, something moving real fast. We still don't have enough data to determine its exact size or e.t.a., but whatever it is, it's big, and it should be here sometime within the next three days."

"How big?"

"Huge. Can't tell for sure yet, but we wouldn't be picking up something that far away unless it was at least a hundred meters across."

"That it?"

"Yes, sir."

"Thanks. Kolanski out." He tapped the line closed. "This day just keeps getting better and better."

He glanced at Margo coldly, then turned back to the comm screen. "Computer, get Admiral Wilson on the line."

Within a few seconds, the admiral's face appeared on the screen. "What can I do for you, Ski?"

"You're not gonna believe this one, Tom. Seems some fanatic, a guy named Callahan..."

"Callahan?" the admiral interrupted. "Rhoury Callahan?"

"Man, am I the only one that doesn't know this freak?" Kolanski muttered.

Admiral Wilson sighed audibly. "That guy's been a constant thorn in my side, always stirring up those cult followers of his."

"Yeah, well, you're going to love this one, Tom. Seems he's got his hands on an old sub, maybe a nuclear warhead too."

"Good Lord. That SOB's going to drop a nuke in the Triangle?"

"Well, actually, we think he's headed for the *Titanic* site."

"What's he got some crazy notion there are aliens *there* now? Man, what a head case."

"Yeah, well..." Kolanski looked sheepishly at the admiral.

"What aren't you telling me, Ski?"

"Maybe it's not such a crazy notion."

"Ski?"

"Look," Kolanski glanced at his watch, "I'll brief you at fourteen hundred – your office. But for now, just get someone on that lunatic's tail, would you?"

"Sure, no problem. Unidentified, unregistered sub in the middle of the Atlantic. This'll be a breeze. I'll get right on it just as soon as I find that needle I dropped in the haystack in my back yard this morning."

"You live in a condo, Tom."

Admiral Tom Wilson smiled. "I've got the Eighth Fleet running maneuvers in the North Atlantic. I'll get them sniffing around."

"Thanks."

"Man, I can't wait to hear your explanation."

"Uh, Admiral?" Margo said from behind Kolanski.

"Who is that, Ski?"

Kolanski turned askew, revealing Margo Feldman to the camera on his monitor. "This is Margo..."

"Feldman," she said.

"She's one of the marine biologists who's been helping us on this," Ski said. Margo beamed with pride. "This is her professor, Blake Richards." He motioned toward Blake, who nodded.

"I think I might be able to help you find that sub," Margo said.

"How's that, young lady?"

"Well, Kenny...that's Kenny Worchanski, one of my coworkers...he said he thought there was a way to ID the sub. He said it was a Gorbachev Class nuclear sub, a relic from the twenty-first century. I don't know a whole lot about subs, but according to Kenny, the Gorbachevs had a real distinctive energy signature, something the Russian Navy developed as a stealth sub. Apparently, this energy signature was so unique it couldn't be recognized as a submarine engine back then, but by today's standards, Kenny said it would be like listening for a Teconean freighter from the rooftop of a spaceport."

The admiral smiled. "That Kenny is one smart cookie."

"He is?" Margo said. "I mean...yeah, he is. One smart cookie."

"Seems our needle's just been magnetized, Ski. Excuse me while I go blow apart a haystack."

"See you at fourteen hundred, Tom."

The monitor blanked out, briefly, and then turned bright blue, with the Space Corps insignia in the center.

Blake glared at Margo. "You're lucky they didn't put you in deep freeze for that stunt."

"Not a bad idea, Richards," Kolanski said coldly.

"That won't be necessary," Blake waved him off. "I'll buckle her into the seat of that plane myself this time."

Margo fidgeted in her chair. "But…"

"Don't even try," Blake snapped.

"Hang on, Richards," Kolanski said. "As much as it pains me, we might need her to get to that kid Kenny if we run into any snags. He's the only insider we got right now."

Blake was shocked. "You mean keep her here? After what she did?"

Ski shook his head. "Yeah, I can't believe I'm saying it either. But… keep her on a short leash, would you?"

"Yes!" Margo blurted out, grinning from ear-to-ear.

– June 5, 2053

My God, it's been twenty years, nearly half my life. The only thing that's kept me sane all this time is the conversations with Nyah. The things he's told me, thoughts I've detailed on these pages over the past decade, have opened my eyes to a way of life once beyond my comprehension, a species advanced millennia beyond us. But all of it is for naught unless I can one day share it with someone other than the despondent souls imprisoned here with me. Knowing this information will die with us makes it all the more painful to endure what we have.

I have tried to persuade Nyah to let us go, to appeal to the sense of righteousness that is so ingrained in the Silesian psyche, but in the end I couldn't supplant my own sense of decency in knowing that our very freedom would spell doom for our Silesian captors. I suppose that shouldn't really bother me, but it does. It's the classic Stockholm Syndrome; I understand that on an intellectual level, I just can't get past it.

Twenty years…what's happened to the world I knew, the people I loved. I might not even recognize what's up there anymore. My dreams are so far distant that I can no longer remember them with any clarity; I was so driven to achieve, but I can't remember why or exactly what it was that I wanted to accomplish. My only goal now is to survive, and even that is such a tenuous thread. What will be there for me when, if, I get back?

The one overriding thought that keeps me going is Rhoury; I can't help but think of all the pain my disappearance must have brought him, and it weighs on me like a crown of thorns wrapped around my heart. Very few can understand the bond between us. I feel like a piece of my soul was torn away by his absence, and I have no doubt that the same torture has plagued him. But I was always the strong one, and I fear for his sanity. I hope he has had the strength to see his way through, and that this journal one day finds its way to him.

- SC

Chapter Eight:
Showdown

The *Minsky* streaked silently through the water, making its way from the Bahamas toward the North Atlantic. The minisub had been designed for a crew of three, but a single crewman could pilot it if his skills were adequate.

Rhoury reached up and pressed his fingers against a picture of his twin sister, Sam, displayed on the viewscreen over the control panel. It showed him standing next to her in full Navy dress, reaching out to place his graduation cap on her as she ducked away, full of laughter. It was the last picture he'd ever taken with her.

A readout on the upper left corner of the main panel caught his eye: *June 5, 2053*, and a somber grunt rattled behind closed lips.

"I got 'em this time Sam," he muttered with resolve.

Rhoury leaned back and smiled serenely as memories of Sam sifted through his mind. The last time he had seen her she was sitting at the bar of the Grand Harbor Hotel in Annapolis, having joined him for a celebratory drink after graduation. She had tried to cajole him into coming along on the traditional family summer vacation, which was to be at a bungalow on a small Bahamian island. Unfortunately, Rhoury had committed to his first tour of duty, which was pretty much set in stone.

He was out on maneuvers when the news reached him. Nobody quite understood why the small pleasure boat had disappeared. It was a beautiful day, calm waters, and his dad was a competent captain, familiar with the seas where he had vacationed several times before. The authorities just chalked it up to another mysterious disappearance in the Bermuda Triangle. *Probably a water funnel*, they had said. But Rhoury knew better.

After Sam's disappearance, Rhoury became obsessed with revenge; somebody had to be responsible. The fact that they never found her body, that he could never get closure, only intensified his drive. He could still feel her presence, and would often awaken in a cold sweat as she cried out to him. The rage nearly drove him insane and he was medically discharged from the Navy.

He used his inheritance to buy a small island near the area where his family had disappeared and founded the New Ocean Society. The more he studied the mystery of the Triangle, the more he became convinced there was an intelligence at work there. In his brilliant but twisted mind there were only two possibilities: a highly evolved aquatic life form indigenous to Earth, or more recent colonization by aliens. He thought it unlikely that an industrialized life form could have developed for centuries on Earth without leaving any other clues. It had to be aliens.

The more he made his case publicly, the more ostracized he had become, until he had withdrawn completely into a world of his own, connected to the outside world only through the website of the New Ocean Society.

*

Commander Farley approached the captain of the battleship *Lord Baltimore*, Jack Syzmanski, whose ever-present five o'clock shadow belied his meticulous demeanor.

"We've reached the designated area, sir."

"Very good. Any sign of the target yet?"

"No, sir."

"Contact the *Calcutta* and see if they are in position."

"Already done, sir. She's ready and waiting."

"Good. Deploy our probes and have *Calcutta* do the same. Program them to surround the target area. I don't want anything getting through. If a clownfish swims past that perimeter, I want to know about it."

"Yes, sir." Farley knew the captain was prone to exaggeration at times, but he understood. They were looking for a twenty-first century minisub, Gorbachev class, with stealth technology. Even with the energy signature codes for the scanners, this would not be easy.

"Let me know when they're in position."

"Yes, sir." The commander saluted.

"Dismissed."

*

Rhoury Callahan had maneuvered the *Minsky* into position about two hours earlier, and shut down the drive engines. The minisub would be tough to spot, but he didn't know the technological capabilities of the aliens.

As he approached the coordinates that Kenny Worchanski had given him, he saw it. The violet hue of the city below slowly came into focus. Rhoury was in awe.

"I knew it!" he said to the walls of the Minsky. "You little buggers were sitting right here under our noses all this time. But what in the hell are you doing up here? I could have searched that damned Triangle for the rest of my life and I would have come up with squat. Do you just send ships down there to do your dirty work, or did you set up little colonies down there too? Maybe little camouflaged colonies, huh? If you had anything like this in the Triangle, I'd have found it by now. Pretty clever to do your hunting so far from home. Pick us off one at a time; planes, boats, whatever wanders by. You snag us, then take us away to study us up here, don't you?"

It briefly crossed his mind that his sister might still be alive, might have been held like a caged animal in the city below all these years. He seethed with anger and suppressed the thought.

"Oh, no. You're not gonna brainwash me; you're not going to get away this time, you bastards."

He armed the warhead, but couldn't purge the thought from his mind. Could she really still be alive? Rhoury decided to lay in wait and scan the colony before he would lay waste to it. The *Minsky* was old, but it had been recently equipped with twenty-sixth century technology. It wouldn't take long to scan for human life forms. If his sister was alive, he would find her. Besides, the information from in-depth scans would prove invaluable in seeking out the hidden colonies in the Triangle.

*

"We've got it, sir," Commander Farley said.

"Excellent. Get the captain of that miniturd on the horn," Syzmanski said.

"Unidentified submarine, this is the naval battleship *Lord Baltimore*. Identify yourself."

Rhoury nearly fell out of his seat. He had been so intent on scanning the ocean floor that he had not noticed the two battleships closing in overhead, much less the dragnet of probes that now surrounded him.

"Great," he muttered to himself.

"Incoming message," the communication computer sounded. "Do you wish to respond?"

"Hell, no," Rhoury seethed through clenched jaws. He kept the comm mic off.

"No response, sir," Farley said to his captain. "Communication link is confirmed, they just don't want to answer."

"They damned sight better," Syzmanski said, walking up to the communications station.

"Unidentified sub, this is Captain Jack Syzmanski, commanding the *Lord Baltimore*. You've got two battleships sitting on your head, and if you do not respond immediately, we're going to blow you out of the water."

"Syzmanski?" Rhoury responded. "Jack Syzmanski? They gave you your own battleship already? Way to go, man."

"Who is that?" Syzmanski asked, looking at the comm screen.

"Couldn't get a video link, sir," Farley said.

"Don't you remember, man? I must have barked at you in the huddle every day for six straight months."

Jack Syzmanski was a junior wide receiver at the Academy the year that Rhoury Callahan led them to the division title.

"Rhoury Callahan?" Jack said, remembering. "I thought you fell off the face of the Earth. What the hell happened to you?"

"The Earth's round, man. Didn't you learn anything in school?"

"Cute, Rhoury. Listen, we've got a situation here. I'm under direct orders from Omnicenter Command to stop you by any means necessary. I don't know what you're up to, but you've got to power down your weapons and surface."

"Omnicenter? How did they know I'd be here?" Rhoury paused briefly, than nodded with enlightenment. "Ah, I get it. You guys knew about the colony all along, didn't you?"

"Colony? What colony?"

"Ah…top secret, huh?"

"What the hell are you talking about, Rhoury."

"C'mon, man. I'm not blind. We're right on top of them."

Syzmanski checked his sensors, which showed nothing but the two battleships, eight probes and the Minsky. "On top of who?"

"You really don't know, do you? I guess they've got some way of blocking surface scans, but I can see them plain as day. Check this out."

Rhoury relayed some of his data on the colony to the *Lord Baltimore*, including a visual uplink.

"What in the…?"

"It's them, Jack. It's the bastards that killed Sam and my parents. You wanted to know where I've been? I've been hunting these SOB's for twenty long years, and now I've got them."

"Look, Rhoury, you've got to back off. If you fire that nuke, it could destabilize the tectonic plates and all hell could break loose."

"If I don't, these little bastards are going to keep multiplying and they're going to keep killing...more and more. I like my chances better with them out of the picture."

"Don't make me do this, Rhoury." Syzmanski signalled to his first officer.

"Surface vessels powering weapons," the Minsky's computer announced. "Would you like to take evasive action?"

"What are you doing, man?"

"Stand down, Rhoury. I don't want to do this."

"I can't, Jack. Not now. Not after all this. I owe it to Sam."

"Sam wouldn't want this, Rhoury. She wouldn't want me to take you down either, but orders are orders."

"You don't have to always follow orders, man. Not when they're wrong."

"They're not wrong. Not this time."

"Look..."

"My God," Jack muttered, eyes still fixed on the viewscreen. "Something's coming up behind you, Rhoury. Check your aft viewer."

Rhoury looked. A large purple sphere was approaching from behind, dancing back and forth in the water so rapidly that any kind of weapons lock would be impossible.

"Looks like you're too late, old friend. They're gonna get me whether you launch your EM charges or not. Give Kathy my love, Jack."

"The Minsky's opening their torpedo bay," Farley said. "Should I fire, sir."

"God dammit, Rhoury…Fire," Jack Syzmanski said dryly.

Rhoury took one last glance at his scanner readout: no human life forms in the structure below. "This one's for you, Sam," he said as he fired the nuclear warhead toward the large sphere at the center of the colony.

The EM charges from the *Lord Baltimore* struck the *Minsky* just after the nuclear warhead launched. The tiny sub shattered just as the spherical ship approached it from behind. The shards from the Minsky's hull pierced the surface of the sphere, sending it aimlessly adrift below the *Lord Baltimore.*

Rhoury Callahan would not live to see the realization of his dream.

*

"It's coming in awfully fast," Kolanski said as he watched the Silesian ship streaking through Earth's solar system on the holographic display in his office. "You sure their intentions are peaceful? It looks like their going to ram us."

"Pretty sure," said Blake, who was sitting around the display with Danny and TC.

"Oh, now that's reassuring," said Danny.

"Look, I've been working on their language, but it's really complex. I'm only at about a four-year old level with it."

"So you know how to tell the Silesians that you have to go potty, huh?"

"Yeah," Blake laughed, "pretty much."

"Great."

"Actually," Blake said, "it's not quite that bad. My Silesian *language* skills may be at a four year old level, but my mind's working just fine. "I got my point across…I think."

"Guess we'll find out."

"You told them we're peaceful, right?" Kolanski asked.

"Yeah."

"And they said they were just coming here to pick up their friends?"

"That was the gist of it, but I can't swear to their level of honesty."

"Well, they're too close for us to use the Defense Shield now anyway. Cross your fingers, gentlemen."

The four men sat around a small table in the center of the room. A holovision projector beamed an image of the approaching vessel into the air between them, where it hovered above the table. The looked on as the ship progressed toward Earth with unabated speed.

"They wouldn't really be stupid enough to ram us with that thing, would they?"

"They wouldn't be the first species to play Kamikaze."

"Sure would be the biggest, though."

They watched as the sphere, three hundred meters in diameter, raced past the moon and toward Earth's atmosphere.

"One way or another, we're going to find out real soon."

They sat silently with bated breath. The Silesian vessel streaked into Earth's atmosphere and came to an abrupt stop about a hundred meters above the surface of the North Atlantic, directly over the alien colony.

"How'd they do that? They can't do that." Danny's fingers were still digging into the arm of the chair. "Can they do that?"

TC released a breath that had been trapped behind clenched teeth. "Apparently."

"Are you talking about braking from near light speed to nothing in a split second, or the fact that they're hovering well below orbital altitude in a vessel that weighs more than Rhode Island?"

"Yes," TC said.

The four men sat motionless, staring at the image in front of them.

*

"Got it, sir," Commander Farley reported on the bridge of the *Lord Baltimore*.

Captain Syzmanski nodded with mixed feelings. He had done what he had to do, but now Rhoury Callahan was gone. A fellow Naval Academy graduate had died at his hands.

"Oh, crap," Farley muttered.

Syzmanski walked up next to Farley and glanced down at the screen showing the images relayed from the undersea probes. The turbulence from the explosion of the *Minsky* had cleared; in the calmness of the deep, a torpedo was streaking directly toward the colony.

"Oh, crap," he muttered.

*

A mere fifteen seconds after the *Minsky* had been blown to pieces, Rhoury Callahan's nuclear warhead struck its target. The torpedo pierced the large sphere in the center of the colony, the remnants of the original ship that had carried the Silesian scientists to Earth nearly six centuries earlier. A few seconds later, the sphere exploded in a mass of bubbles and debris, mushrooming out and accelerating toward the surface, erupting in a tidal wave that engulfed the helpless *Lord Baltimore* and her sister ship, the *Calcutta*, sending them to rest silently on the bottom of the ocean next to the wreckage of the Titanic.

Chapter Nine:
Erasure

The metallic blue orb hung over the ocean like an ethereal moon. For centuries, Silesian ships had been scouring this quadrant of space, looking for any sign of what may have happened to the ancient expedition.

The vastness of Earth's oceans were intriguing, but for those who had monitored the violence of the planet's inhabitants, it was clearly too dangerous to risk contact. Scout ships remained at a safe distance, and it was only by chance that one passed close enough to pick up the weak distress signal. Authorization to intervene came quickly.

As the sphere scanned the waters for signs of Silesian life, its captain witnessed the surging waterspout below. Sensors confirmed the worst; debris spewing from the ocean was filled with Silesian technology, and worse yet, organic material from Silesian bodies.

*

Kolanski made his way to Space Corp's communication center, with Richards and Stryker close behind. The young lieutenant on duty stood at attention as he saw them enter.

"At ease, Lieutenant."

"Thank you, sir." Lieutenant Harry Meyers stood awkwardly, not quite at attention, but certainly not at ease.

"Relax, son. Have you been monitoring the situation in the Atlantic?"

"Yes, sir."

"Good. I need you to establish a link with those bastards."

"I've been trying, sir." Meyers looked fidgety. "I can't seem to get a fix on their communications. Whatever they're using, it's not like anything I've seen before. They use a similar subspace carrier signal, but it's just random noise, nothing the computer can pin down."

"Mind if I give it a try?" Blake asked.

Lieutenant Meyers eyed the civilian, then looked back to Kolanski.

"It's OK, Lieutenant."

Meyers backed away from the comm station and handed his earpiece to Blake.

"Thanks," Blake said, taking it and pulling up a chair. He lifted the earpiece to the side of his head, where it scanned the contours of his ear, and suspended itself a half centimeter from his auditory canal.

Meyers nodded and moved over to the adjacent panel, where the Space

Corps computer was scanning the Silesian vessel and displaying tactical data.

"They've backed off to an altitude of 12,480 meters, sir…they're powering weapons!"

"What kind of fire power?"

"Unknown, sir. But the way they zipped in here…man, with that kind of technology, we're in deep sh…" Meyers made a feeble attempt at clearing his throat, "uh, trouble, sir."

Ski glanced over at the sensor display. "You've got to talk some sense into these…fish people, or whatever they are," he said to Blake.

"Look, I can barely…"

"Whatever you come up with, it's a heck of a lot better than anything else we got."

Blake stepped up to the comm panel and programmed in the frequency used for the distress call that had been intercepted aboard the Woods Hole shuttle, the same frequency that *Stargazer* had intercepted in deep space. The next thing that came out of Blake's mouth was a piercing series of clicks and squeals sending everyone else in the room scrambling to cover their ears.

Stryker winced. "What the heck was that?"

"Sorry guys," Blake said. "There was no time to program the language database into the computer. I had to try to imitate their language verbally."

"Sounds like a damned parrot," Lieutenant Meyers said, still rubbing his ears.

"More like a dolphin, actually," Blake said, "but with a wider range of intonation and duration variability."

"Yeah. Whatever," Meyers mumbled.

"I also had to account for how it'll sound inside the alien ship. See, when the sound hits the liquid atmosphere they live in, the waveforms will be altered just like when you try to talk while swimming underwater. Only without knowing the viscosity and exact composition of their liquid atmosphere, it's impossible to predict just how the sound waves will act. In fact, if you take into account…"

"Who gives a rat's ass," Danny barked. "They're gonna blow us up while you're babbling on about sound waves. Just say 'We come in peace' before they fire on us, would ya?"

"That's basically what I told them, or at least I tried to. All we can do now is wait for a reply. Hopefully, I got my message across. Maybe I should repeat it."

"No!" All three men shouted at the same time.

The comm system signaled an incoming message.

"Colonel?" Meyers looked toward Kolanski.

"Put it through, son."

"Yes, sir."

Lieutenant Meyers activated the transmission, which sounded just as bizarre as the clicks and squeals Blake had just sent out.

Kolanski winced. "Can you make anything out of that, Blake?"

"Most of it. It seems that they are willing to listen to us, but they're pretty pissed about us blowing up their colony."

"No kidding," Danny muttered.

"The alien vessel is powering down weapons, sir," Meyers said.

Kolanski breathed a sigh of relief. "All right, then. Here's what we're going to do. Blake, I want you to tell them…"

"Colonel," Blake interrupted, "if I can make a suggestion?"

Kolanski nodded.

"If I download the data from my computer into the Space Corps universal translator it should make things a lot easier. We can speak English, the Silesians can speak their language and you'll be able to communicate directly without depending on my rough translations. Besides, I think everyone will be a lot happier around here without me squawking at the computer."

Kolanski tipped his head. "Get on it."

"Yes, sir." Blake turned and unleashed another barrage of squeals toward the comm panel.

Danny's hands shot up to cover his ears. "*Man,*" he hissed through clenched teeth "I thought you said you weren't going to do that."

"Sorry. Just trying to buy us some time."

Kolanski said, "Let Lieutenant Meyers here handle the download. Nothing gets into the Space Corps computers without clearing multiple layers of firewalls. If it's not done right, you'll never get the translator working."

Blake nodded. "Let's get to work, Lieutenant."

"Right."

*

While the two men were programming Space Corps' universal translator with the Silesian language, Kolanski took the opportunity to brief his Commander-in-Chief.

President Atkinson and General Burnstone, the ranking commander of Federation forces, were engaged in tense negotiations at a summit meeting in North America with a Teconean delegation when the call came in. He requested a brief recess.

In spite of the gravity of the situation with the Silesians, the President could not break away without risking a set-back with the hot-blooded Teconeans; he sent Burnstone back to handle negotiations with the Silesians.

*

Within an hour, Space Corp's universal translator was handling the new language with 98% accuracy.

The voice of the Silesian captain came out in English. "We demand to know the circumstances that led to the destruction of our colony."

"We are still working out the details ourselves, Captain," Kolanski said. "We were not aware of the existence of the colony until today. It seems that a terrorist intercepted our communications and attacked your colony before we could stop him."

"Terrorist?"

"Terrorist… a criminal who does not follow the rules of our society; one who lashes out with violence rather than seeking a diplomatic solution."

"And you allow this kind of behavior on your world?"

"No. That is, not when we can stop it. But this is a big world; we can't control everyone."

"Your civilization is barbaric, Colonel."

"Not at all. It's just that we value freedom above all else, and in order to preserve freedom, security is sometimes vulnerable. You can't have absolute security in a free society."

"You certainly can, Colonel Kolanski, if you make it a priority."

"And you think invading our world is not an act of barbarism?"

"We are here on a rescue mission, Colonel."

"And what about that colony of yours? By our calculations, they've been here some six hundred years. Who were they here to rescue?"

"Our colony was there strictly for scientific purposes. They were on a mission to observe new worlds, but they became lost to us centuries ago. They were presumed dead. It only recently came to our attention that they had survived and were stranded on your world. We came to extract them as soon as we became aware of their existence. But now, you have made that impossible."

"Sir!" Meyers interrupted. "They are powering weapons again."

"Captain," Kolanski pleaded with the alien, "We're a peaceful race. I'm as appalled as you by the attack on your colony."

"I think not, Colonel. We are detecting several well-armed ships heading in our direction."

"They're only there for self-defense, Captain," Kolanski said. "I'll tell them to hold their positions." He nodded toward Meyers, motioning for him to signal the fleet. Within seconds, the geographic display in front of them showed the fleet holding fifty miles from their target.

"You will tell them to pull back."

"But what assurance do I have…"

"They will pull back or be destroyed."

Kolanski fumed. He gave the signal for the ships to pull back.

"Alien weapons still armed," Meyers said.

"Captain,…" Kolanski started, but was quickly interrupted by the alien.

"We learned long ago that primitive terrestrials were not to be trusted. Only a fool ignores history."

"That's not *our* history, Captain."

"None-the-less, I will take no chances."

The heavy steel and glass door to the comm room slid open with a loud *whoosh*, cutting into the tension. Everyone turned in unison as General Burnstone walked in.

"Sir," Kolanski and Meyers saluted.

"At ease, gentlemen. Where are we at?"

Kolanski quickly briefed him.

Burnstone turned toward the comm panel. "Captain," he said to the Silesian leader, "this is General Burnstone. I have a solution."

"You can not bring our colonists back, General. There is no solution."

"Ah, but perhaps we can, Captain. Perhaps we can."

"But, General," Kolanski started.

Burnstone raised a hand in Ski's direction, then continued on with his conversation. "We have the means to send a vessel back in time to intercept your first ship. If we knew what went wrong and exactly when it went wrong, we could send back help and avoid the catastrophe before it happens. They will never have been stranded here in the first place, and their deaths will have never occurred."

This was met by silence from the alien vessel.

Ski motioned to Lieutenant Meyers to cut off outgoing communications. "But General," he said in a loud whisper, "the President and Congress have strictly forbidden the use of the time-warp system. You know that. The risk of altering the past…"

"Is what, Ski? Greater than the risk of an alien warship with vastly superior weapons and a captain hell-bent on revenge? I think I'll take my chances with time-warp. Besides, it looks like it kind of spooked him, don't you think?"

They both looked at the comm station in anticipation.

The reply came slowly. "You…you have the ability to do this?"

Myer's looked up from his station. "Alien vessel powering down weapons, sir."

Burnstone smiled at Ski. "We don't use it casually, Captain, but it's very effective when needed."

"Most interesting," the Silesian captain said. "And you would be willing to share this technology with us?"

"No, sir. We can't do that. I'm sure you understand. But we can use it to rescue your colonists."

"Let me confer with my staff on this matter, General. We will reply to your generous offer shortly."

"At your leisure, Captain."

Burnstone motioned for Meyers to cut off the outgoing signal once again. "Keep a twenty-four hour watch on this thing, son. I hope you like coffee, because I can't afford to let anyone else in here for a while. Even *you* shouldn't know about the time-warp system."

"Then it *does* exist, sir? I thought that story was just a rumor."

"As far as you're concerned, it is." Burnstone raised an eyebrow.

"Yes, sir." Lieutenant Meyers slumped back in his chair as he watched Burnstone turn and walk away.

"Ski, Richards, Stryker…you're with me," Burnstone snapped as he headed out the door.

"Oh, and Stryker," the general said, spinning around suddenly.

The three men trailing closely at his heels nearly bumped into him.

"Yes, sir?"

"Get that wife of yours on the horn." No one knew the time-warp system better than Jennifer Lee.

"Yes, sir." Stryker normally wasn't much for protocol, but General Burnstone was larger than life, the kind of man who could walk into a room and command respect, even a bit of fear, merely by his presence. It was not easy to intimidate Danny Stryker, but Burnstone came close.

It was a short walk from the Space Corps Communications Center to the R&D labs where Quigley spent most of his time. The professor was standing in the middle of his main lab when the four men entered.

"Ah, General," Quigley said with his usual sardonic tone, "slumming it today? I haven't seen you down in the bowels of R&D for months."

Burnstone ignored the comment. "Professor, I believe you know Captain Stryker and Colonel Kolanski. This is Dr. Blake Richards, from Woods Hole."

Richards walked up to the professor, extending his right hand.

"Woods Hole, huh? What brings you to the other side of the wilderness, Dr. Richards?" As they reached out to shake, Quigley's hand passed right through Blake's, and he bellowed with child-like laughter.

"Incredible," Blake whispered, reaching out and running his hand back and forth through Quigley's body, which shimmered briefly with each pass-through. "How did you get this kind of resolution? This thing's is better than a holosuit."

"Darned right," Quigley said, walking up behind them. He tapped a button on a large wristband, and the hologram faded away. "You have to *wear* those things; a distinct disadvantage if somebody starts shooting at you. I'll take this little gizmo over a holosuit anytime. Same realism, but you can be a hundred meters away when the weapons start discharging."

"Awesome," Blake said.

Quigley studied him strangely for a brief moment, and then a smile slowly crept across his face.

Blake stepped back uncomfortably.

"Yeah, yeah," Danny muttered. "Enough with the Mutual Admiration Society."

"Right," General Burnstone agreed. "Let's get to it, gentlemen." He turned to Quigley. "Is there some place private we can talk?"

Quigley held up his hands, gesturing around the room. "No one comes into my lab without me knowing it, General. And as for eavesdropping, I guarantee you this is the safest place in Omnicenter." A grin slowly crept across his face, and with a gleam in his eye, he added "even safer than your office."

Burnstone eyed him closely. "We can talk about that one later. Get me to a comm station. There's something you need to see."

Quigley directed the group over to a large table in the middle of the lab.

"Computer, activate image screen," he said.

A beam of soft blue light rose from the center of the table, forming a three dimensional elliptical view screen about two meters long, one meter wide and one meter high.

"I use this for teaching," Quigley said. He pressed a button on the tabletop and six seats slid out around the periphery, three on each side. "Have a seat, gentlemen."

They settled in around the display. The four men stared at Quigley, who shrugged his shoulders.

"It's your show, General."

"Right," Burnstone said. "Computer: voice pattern recognition: Burnstone."

"Acknowledged, General Burnstone," the computer answered.

"Activate live image from the Space Corps Comm Center receiver."

An image appeared of the alien sphere hanging over the Atlantic. Without the now obliterated naval ships in the water below, there was no frame of reference to judge the size of the vessel.

"Display reference grid in three dimensions" Quigley said.

A red grid came up over the display, calibrated in meters.

"Good Lord!" Quigley yelped. "Where did that come from?"

"God knows," Burnstone said.

"The real question you should be asking," Danny said, "is what's it doing *here*?"

"I'm not sure I want to know," Quigley said.

"Yes. You do," Burnstone said tersely, and then turned to Blake. "Richards, why don't you take it from here? You seem to know more about this than anyone in the Corps."

"Now that's reassuring," Danny piped in.

Blake began to describe the events of the past few days, but Quigley soon interrupted. "Silesians…so that's what they call themselves."

"You know about them?"

Quigley's lips curled in. "The destroyers of Ariana."

"But how…?"

"Let's just say I became good friends with the Starscape probe when they needed my help to keep it from destroying the Teconean Empire…not that that would have been a *bad* thing." Then, he added with a twinkle in his eye, "But I *am* surprised *you* know about it."

Blake shifted uneasily in his seat.

"Can we save the cat and mouse game for later, gentlemen?" Danny interrupted.

Quigley's gaze hadn't shifted from Blake. "By all means."

Blake finished filling him in.

"So," Quigley said, "sounds like we're in it pretty deep, huh?"

"Yup," Danny said. "And now they've got some kind of big humungous butt-kickng weapon pointed right down our throats with their finger on the trigger. So…you can fix this, right?"

For one of the few times in recent memory, Quigley was speechless.

"That's OK, professor. Take your time. We've got…" Danny looked down at his watch, "oh, I'd say about…a couple minutes or so before they attack."

"If I had some data on the Silesian technology, I may be able to…"

"We already have a plan, Professor," General Burnstone said. "We just need you to make it work. We need you to equip the *Stargazer* with a time-warp generator."

A voice broke in from across the room. "Sounds like my cue," Jennifer Lee said as she strode in with TC by her side.

"God, you're not sending us back to the Old West again, are you?" TC asked, rubbing his thighs. "If I never see another horse, it'll be too soon."

"TC!" Kolanski greeted his old friend with a broad grin. "How ya feeling?"

"Not so bad, actually. This thing," he pointed to his new bionic eye, "is incredible. I'm still getting used to some of the distortion, but I can see stuff I've never seen before." He winked at Blake, who shot a nervous glance in Quigley's direction.

"Good to see you, buddy," Danny said as he stood and gave his partner a slap on the back. "Ready to do some time-warping?"

"God, no," TC muttered. "One bout of time-jump nausea was more than enough, thank you."

Danny laughed. "He's ready. What've you got in mind for the Stargazer, General?"

"As soon as Quigley gets her ready to fly, you two are taking her back to 1912 to rescue the original Silesian ship before it crashes. We'll get rid of these bastards before they ever get here."

Burnstone stared at Quigley. "Only thing is, you've got to get the *Stargazer* ready to go before the Silesians get impatient. If they blow us up before we can launch, we'll never have the chance to change history."

Quigley looked up at Jennifer. "You've got great timing, Major Lee," he said to his former research assistant.

"Thanks, boss," she smiled, then panned over to Danny and gave him a wink.

"This is the lady you want to talk to, gentlemen," Quigley said. "I can bore you silly with time-warp theory, but Jennifer here is the only one who's ever installed a time-warp field generator in a ship before. At least," he said, with obvious reference to the traitorous Hans Beck, "the only one we can trust."

"And it was the *Stargazer* I installed it in. It'll be a breeze, guys. Just give me a few days."

"You have twelve hours, Major," the general said. "We launch at oh-eight hundred."

"But I need time to recalibrate…"

"Twelve hours," the general repeated. "Myers just heard from the Silesians." He glanced down at the screen on his watch. "They've given us until noon tomorrow to resolve this thing. We have exactly sixteen hours to undo the past. That's all they're giving us, and we're in no position to bargain. We launch by oh-eight hundred. That gives you a four-hour margin of error in case anything goes wrong. By noon tomorrow, their colony is brought back to life, or Earth comes under attack."

The room was silent for a moment as they each digested the ramifications of their mission.

Quigley broke the tension. "I saved most of the components, Jennifer," he said. "It should be no problem if we work together."

"You what!" Kolanski barked at Quigley. "You were under strict orders to destroy all evidence of the time-warp generator other than secure program files."

"And ain't you glad I didn't, fellas," Quigley smiled at Colonel Kolanski and at General Burnstone, who just shook his head.

"You're one in a million, Quigley," Burnstone said, adding under his breath, "Thank God."

Burnstone and Kolanski stood up to leave. "Richards, Stryker, McGee…you're with us. These folks have some work to do," Burnstone said.

No one argued. They followed the general out the door, with Danny stealing a quick kiss from Jennifer along the way.

Chapter Ten:
When in the Course of Human Events...

General Burnstone was glad to be home. In spite of the crisis at hand, any excuse that pried him away from the Teconeans was a good one in his estimation. He tolerated the Neanderthals only when he had to, and every time he met with them he thanked his lucky stars that his ancestors had the foresight to banish the burly creatures to Teconea back in the early days of hyperspatial travel. It was rare to see one on Earth these days.

Burnstone's office was not far from the Hall of Presidents, where President Atkinson and the presidents of each of the human outworlds had their formal government offices. Many of the officials lived in the residential wing of the Hall during their time on Earth, but Burnstone's wife had refused the invitation, much to his chagrin. In the end, he decided it would be far easier to deal with the commute than a dissatisfied wife. He settled for a comfortable overstuffed crimson sofa that sat in the corner of his office across from a picture window looking out over a courtyard dotted with small trees, a popular lunch spot for office staffers on temperate African afternoons.

"Gentlemen," he said, motioning Danny, TC, Blake and Ski into his office as the door swung open.

Danny headed straight for the sofa and plopped down comfortably. "Nice," he said, settling back. "Sure beats those plastic discs we were sitting on down in R&D."

TC settled in on the other end of the sofa with an "ahh," while Burnstone and Blake sat in the two facing armchairs across the coffee table. Kolanski, the last one in, winced and settled for the empty spot on the sofa between Stryker and McGee.

"Glad you're comfortable, gentlemen, " Burnstone muttered, "'cause you're about to be thrown into one whale of a ride."

Danny smiled. "I get it."

Burnstone glared in his direction. "Get what?"

"Whale...very funny, sir."

The general's expression didn't break. "I don't do funny, Stryker."

The smile faded from Danny's face, with a subtle clearing of the throat.

"General," Blake said, "if I may."

Burnstone nodded.

"No disrespect intended, sir, but I believe there's a major flaw in your plan."

Blake hesitated, waiting for a rebuke from the imposing general, but none came. Burnstone was a decisive man, but not a foolish one. He had Blake in his office for a reason.

"I'm listening."

"I have reason to believe the original Silesian ship that crashed here in the twentieth century may be what sank the Titanic."

The general raised an eyebrow. "How in God's name did you come up with that?"

"Well, you see, I've been monitoring..."

"Blake?" Danny glared.

He hesitated briefly, then went on, keeping the explanation short and to the point.

"Interesting theory, Richards," the general said. "Maybe it's right and maybe it's not, but what does that have to do with our problem?"

"Well, a lot of very prominent people died when the *Titanic* went down, sir."

"Ahh," the general nodded, "so if we go back there and stop it from happening...."

"We'll change our past," Ski finished the thought. "We've got to intercept the Silesians *after* the *Titanic* goes down."

"But then how do we stop them from getting stranded on Earth?" Danny asked. "By then, the damage was already done."

"We'll just have to help them fix their ship," Blake said.

"And how do you propose to do that. You an expert on Silesian technology?"

"No. But I know where to find someone who is," Blake said.

"So we just ask them for a repair kit to take back in time with us?"

"Yup."

"And how are they going to know what to send. They can't very well ask the colonists, now can they?"

"Those colonists probably sent a lot more than a distress call when they raised the mother ship. I suspect our new guests know precisely what happened in that crash and how to fix it, they just don't want to admit it."

A facetious laugh erupted from TC's lips. "No kiddin'. That would make those bastards look guilty of the very thing they're accusing us of – destroying a ship full of civilians."

"Exactly, but I think I've got enough information to convince them we already know, and once we get that out of the way they can admit they know what's needed for the repairs."

Burnstone rubbed his cheek. "So they give us the parts and we deliver them."

"That's the plan. The colonists fix their ship and leave Earth right after the crash."

"Then how will we know anything about them?" TC asked. "Once we get back, it'll be like they were never here, other than the Titanic, which we'll never think to pin on them. The mother ship won't have had any reason to come and we won't even know those bastards are out there. We'll be sitting ducks if they ever decide to come back."

"But won't *you* remember?" Kolanski asked. "When you come back to the future, won't you remember what you've changed?"

"Of course we will," Danny said, then frowned. "At least I think so. Hell, we tried so damned hard *not* to change anything last time, there wouldn't have been anything to remember."

"Well," TC shrugged, "even if we *had* changed something, we wouldn't realize it if we had forgotten about it by the time we got back, now would we?"

The room fell silent, everyone staring blankly at each other.

"Who the hell cares?" the general finally said. "As long as that damned sphere isn't sitting out there pointing its weapons at us when you get back."

"Though it would be pretty cool to see what they've got," Danny said.

The general stared stone-faced at Danny.

"Well," Danny said, slapping his hands against his thighs and standing up to leave, "I guess we'd better get working on our plan, huh guys?"

The other men got up.

"McGee, you escort Dr. Richards back over to the comm center. I want you two to contact the Silesians and tell them to prepare whatever it is we'll need to take back to their damaged ship in the twentieth century, and tell them I'm sending a battleship from the Atlantic fleet out to make the pick up."

"Yes, sir." McGee said.

"When you're finished in the comm station, rejoin these two over in the colonel's office and finalize a plan."

He looked Kolanski squarely in the eyes. "I want a briefing as soon as you've got something."

"Yes, sir," Kolanski said.

Ski and TC saluted, and Stryker weakly mimicked the gesture. Blake's hand twitched ever so slightly, as he suppressed the response that had been so deeply ingrained in his psyche some three hundred years earlier.

The general snapped back his salute, and the four men turned to leave the room.

*

Within an hour, Kolanski was on his way back to Burnstone's office. The general was sitting behind his oversized mahogany desk, catching up on the sports highlights playing on his desktop screen.

A pleasant chirp sounded from his monitor.

"Damn," he muttered to himself.

"Intercom on."

The sounds of crowd noise from the basketball game faded as the video feed continued. In the lower right corner, a window popped up with the stoic face of a woman, forty-something with short brunette hair and hazel eyes. Doris had been working for the general for so long that she had acquired an uncanny knack for mimicking his gruff demeanor; an almost comical trait that was invisible to the two of them.

"What is it, Doris?" The general sighed as he watched Billy Wilson sink a thirty-foot jumper behind her face.

"Colonel Kolanski to see you, sir," she sighed back.

"Already?" Burnstone's brow furrowed. "Send him in."

Doris's face faded from the screen as a firm knock sounded at the door. "Come."

Kolanski opened the door and peered in.

"Ski." The general motioned him in.

Kolanski entered and sat in one of the two matching mahogany armchairs facing the desk.

"We've got our plan, sir."

Chapter Eleven:
Volatile Cargo

Even the morning sun was denied entrance to Landing Bay A-17, where the *Stargazer* was being prepped for her mission.

Though Omnicenter's Spaceport was the most advanced in the Federation, it was arguably the dreariest, devoid of all color but military gray and blue. A seemingly endless array of blacktopped roads weaved their way through a maze of rectangular, steel-blue buildings, most of which housed landing bays for the Space Corps' elite ships. On the non-descript rooftops, fluorescent yellow numbers painted inside a square of the same color were impregnated with luminite crystals, assuring that each was clearly visible from the night sky.

Section A was comprised of a small group of hangers near the edge of the complex adjoining the Command Center. Rooftops in this area were devoid of the bold markings, instead embedded with discreet microtransmitters capable of recognizing authorized ships and assuming navigation control, coordinating the descent through the landing bay roof, which would be opened just long enough to accomplish the task.

Hanger A-17 was where the *Stargazer* had first been fit with a time-warp generator, and for Jennifer, it was a sentimental favorite. No one outside Quigley's staff had access, and it was kept as spotless as their labs.

"Whew!" Danny whistled, walking into the hanger from the well-guarded hallway. "This place is cleaner than our house."

Jennifer, already aboard, peeked out from behind the entry door at the top of a short flight of stairs. She wiped the sweat off her brow with the back of her hand and tossed her long silky hair out of her eyes with an accomplished wave of the head.

"Of course it is," she said. "*You* haven't been in here yet."

Danny started to protest, then just shrugged and turned to TC, who had entered behind him. "When she's right, she's right."

TC smiled.

Jennifer hopped down off the last step and gave the *Stargazer* a gentle slap on the hull. "She's all set."

"Great," Danny said. "The sooner the better. Burnstone will be all over our backs if we don't lift off by oh-eight hundred."

"Tell me about it," Jennifer said. "The hanger crew should have all of the supplies loaded up in another twenty minutes or so. That'll give me just enough time to clean up and grab my gear. We should be off Earth within the hour."

"We?" Danny eyed her suspiciously. "What's this *we*, kemosabe?"

"Oh, come on." Jennifer turned her eyes skyward. "You're not going to start that again, are you?"

"Look, Jen. You know how this time travel stuff goes. The less we mess with things, the better. We don't want anyone back there we don't need. TC, Blake and I can handle things just fine."

"Oh, yeah?"

"Yeah."

"And just which one of you is going to fix the time-warp relays if they go off-line?" She stared Danny right in the eyes.

He looked down.

"Uh-huh. I thought so." Jennifer tossed her hair back off her face again, triumphantly. "See you in an hour, boys."

TC nodded ever so slightly as she walked by.

"Got her wrapped right around your little finger, eh, dude?"

Danny grinned. "You betcha."

"Right."

"Hey. If *you* were married to her, wouldn't *you* want her coming along?"

"Good point."

Danny laughed. "Come on," he said, hoisting his pack back up on his shoulder, "Let's get our gear on board and prep for take-off."

The two men climbed the steps as they had done hundreds of times before, and disappeared into the ship. Blake was already aboard, programming the Silesian language into the communications system.

The sultry voice of the ship's computer greeted Danny as he entered. "Hello, Captain Stryker."

"How're you doing, darlin'," he answered.

Blake looked up and shook his head. "I still can't believe you talk to your ship like that."

"Hey," Danny said to Blake, "I'd think you, of all people, would understand."

Blake looked up. "You're not seriously comparing me to your computer?"

"Well," Danny said sheepishly. "I mean...I just figured maybe you'd get the connection I have with her, you know? We go way back, that old computer and me. She's saved my butt more times than I can count."

"Who are you calling old, Captain Stryker?" the computer said, sounding offended.

"Sorry, darlin'," Danny apologized. "Just an expression. Now pay attention to Blake, here. We're going to need you to communicate with those fish-people when we get to them, and the more you know, the better."

"I *can* do more that one thing at a time, Captain."

Danny shook his head and smiled, then helped TC prep for take-off while Blake finished up.

*

Jennifer poked her head through the entrance door to the bridge. "You boys about ready?"

"Back already?" Danny asked, looking at his watch.

"One hour," Jennifer announced. "As promised."

"Course laid in," TC said. "Let's get this show on the road."

"Buckle up boys and girls," Danny said as he swung into the pilot seat. "God, I love this part." He reached forward and activated the power-up cycle for the main engines.

TC was seated beside him at the tactical display, where navigation and communication could be accessed, as well as the main weapons controls. The *Stargazer* was not designed for battle, but even a merchant ship needed defensive capabilities out on the fringes of Federation territory. Blake was seated at the auxiliary station in the back of the small bridge, where he could access the communications computer when needed.

"I'd love to," Jennifer said wryly, "but just where would you suggest I sit?"

Danny patted his lap and smiled.

"Yeah, right. In your dreams."

"I guess you should have installed an extra chair while you were putting in the time-warp generator."

"Sure," Jennifer said, slapping her forehead. "Why didn't I think of that? And I had all that time to kill."

"Why don't you secure yourself in at the desk chair in my quarters," Danny said. "The monitor there will give you access to engineering so you can keep an eye on the warp systems."

"Always trying to find a way to talk me into the bedroom, aren't you?" She winked and turned to go back to his quarters.

"Are you blushing, Ace?" TC asked. "I think you're blushing."

"He's definitely blushing," Blake said.

"All right, all right. Just hold onto something."

Danny smacked the control panel to engage the engines, but the *Stargazer* lifted off the landing pad as gently as always, the motion barely perceptible to its passengers. She glided out of the spaceport parallel to the ground, then once clear, accelerated skyward, pushing her crew gently back into their seats. They sat silently, admiring the view of Earth shrinking away behind them.

A few moments later, the ship's computer broke the silence. "We have obtained orbital altitude."

"Right. Engage trajectory and velocity to maintain present orbit."

"Acknowledged."

The computer fine-tuned the ship's orbit so precisely that no motion was apparent within her walls.

"How long will it take to plot the time jump, Jen?"

"About five minutes," she answered through the comm. "If you boys want to stretch your legs, do it now. You'll want to be secured in nice and tight when the time jump is engaged."

Vivid memories of the last jump swarmed in TC's mind. "You ain't kidding,"

The three men stayed in their seats, concentrating on their respective roles in the upcoming mission.

Danny had been ordered to pilot the *Stargazer* to the site of the *Titanic* one month after the sinking, to assure that no one would spot them, and then deliver a package of items needed for repairs that had been prepared by the future Silesians. He had tried to convince Burnstone they should arrive before the crash to keep those damned fish-people off the planet, but the general wasn't willing to risk exposure.

I mean it, Stryker, he'd said. *That's an order.*

Danny had answered with a salute, knowing that once the mission started and he was out of communication range, he could always claim field command prerogative to alter the mission. He also knew the general would expect that.

The general would be right.

*

"Ready," Jennifer announced.

"Good," TC said, fidgeting with the tactical display. He was anxious to get this over with…the jump *and* the mission.

"We're all set in here, Jen," Danny said.

Jennifer triggered the reactor that powered the time-warp generator. A barely audible hum was heard throughout the ship.

"Ready when you are," her voice came through the comm.

"I'm never gonna be ready," TC muttered, grasping the arms of his chair and digging his fingernails in so hard they turned white.

Danny smiled, and tapped a series of commands into his panel.

"Time-warp system activated," the computer announced. "On your mark, Captain."

The jump could have been triggered with one more tap, but Danny preferred to initiate by voice command. He gripped his armrests firmly.

"Engage."

A wave of dizziness and nausea swept over the crew of the Stargazer. It lasted only a matter of seconds, but the aftereffects lingered as they sat silently in their seats waiting for the discomfort to pass. TC was the first to muster up the energy to speak.

"Geez, doc," he said to Jennifer through the comm system, "can't you do something about that?"

"Gimme a break," she muttered back, still feeling the effects herself. "It's not cool enough that I just transported you back in time six centuries, now you want me to make it more comfy for you?"

"Not such a bad idea if you ask me," Danny said as he shifted in his seat.

Blake grinned. "Bunch of wimps."

"Just get the scans going while the rest of us get our stomachs back out of our throats," Danny said.

Blake activated the ship's scanners, and a series of numbers and star charts began to light up the monitors.

"April 14, 1912. Perfect. I think we're in business, lady and gentle-men."

"Gee," TC said. "You mean we don't get to do that again?"

"Oh, yeah," Jen added. "We do it again real soon. That is, unless you want to stay back here in the industrial age."

"I've got to think about that one awhile, doc," he said.

The forward viewscreen showed a pitch-black sky. Danny had plotted the jump to place the *Stargazer* at a suborbital altitude two hundred miles from the crash site, a distance that would keep them safely out of the entry trajectory of the Silesian vessel. Although Danny was unsure exactly when or where the alien ship had first landed, he knew its exact location when the *Titanic* went down…assuming Blake's theory was correct.

"You'd better be right about this, Blake. It'd be a hell of a thing if that Silesian ship smacks into *us* instead of the Titanic."

"Well," TC said, "at least we'd change history."

"Yeah, and we wouldn't have to worry about *how* we changed it, seeing that we'd be on the bottom of the ocean and all."

"Good point."

"Look!" Blake pointed at the view screen.

The fiery Silesian sphere was directly in front of them, streaking through the atmosphere.

"It's beautiful," Jennifer whispered.

"Sure is," Danny agreed. "Those poor bastards on the *Titanic* probably think they're seeing a shooting star rather than a fireball that's about to send them all to hell. What do the scanners show, Blake?"

"Nothing; at least no crash. Scans indicate the sphere made a controlled landing on the water's surface."

"No crash?"

"Nope."

"Where's the Titanic?"

The image on the viewscreen showed little detail in the blackness of the night. They couldn't make out the sphere, but the lights of the *Titanic* were beautiful.

"There she is. A little over three miles from the sphere on a collision course."

"Zoom in on the sphere's location and enhance," Danny said.

TC tapped on the panel in front of him and details started to emerge on the viewscreen as he used sensor data to enhance the image.

"What the hell is that? Are you sure that's them?"

The alien ship bobbed in the water, but the spherical form was marred by jagged spikes protruding in a seemingly random pattern.

"Who else would it be?"

As they looked on, the form gradually morphed into a pyramidal pattern with irregular peaked formations jutting out from its base.

"What is that, some sort of holoimage?"

TC checked his sensors, then shook his head. "Ice. They're covering themselves with ice."

"Camouflage," Jennifer muttered.

"Of course," Blake said. "Just another iceberg in the sea to anyone who happens to spot them."

"Like the Titanic?"

TC nodded and zoomed the image back out so they could see the position of both vessels.

"Still on collision course. Now less than three miles and closing."

"So why aren't the Silesians taking evasive action?"

"Beats me," Blake shrugged. "They've got to know she's there."

"Why are they always *she*?" Jennifer asked.

"Huh?" Danny asked.

"Why do men always refer to their ships as 'she'?"

"Cause we worship them," TC said, matter-of-factly.

Jennifer stopped and thought for a second. "Good answer. It's a good thing *you* spoke first, because I bet one of these other clowns would have come up with something a little more…colorful."

"*Moi?*" Danny chirped.

Jennifer ignored him and studied the scans. "They've still got power. Maybe their scanners are off-line while they're crystallizing the outside of their hull. If they knew the *Titanic* was heading their way, they'd stop whatever they're doing and get out of there."

"So they're basically floating blind? Great system. Is that the kind of technological wizardry we're up against?"

"Every system has its flaws," Jennifer said. "Even a Teconean starfighter can be defeated by a ship like this if you know where to strike." History had proven her point. "For them," Jennifer motioned toward the screen, "it's probably just a few minutes of blindness in the vastness of the sea. What are the odds they'd run into an object large enough to do them any damage in that amount of time."

"Pretty high, in this case," TC said.

The room fell silent. Up until now, it had been like watching a movie, observing a moment in history that had been recorded for posterity. But as they looked on, the reality of the situation overwhelmed them; they weren't observing history, they were living it. And every single one of them knew they had the power to change what was about to occur.

Jennifer's head dropped. "Too high," she whispered into the air.

They all sat silently and waited for the inevitable.

She began to pace back and forth in front of the viewscreen. Her fists clenched tighter with each turn; the slap of her shoes betrayed by a rhythmic clang resonating from the metal deck.

"Enough!" Danny stopped her with an outstretched arm.

She uncoiled at him. "For God's sake! We can't just sit here and do nothing."

"Jen," he took her firmly by the arms and fixed on her gaze, "we have no choice."

"There's always a choice."

"And what? Risk the lives of everyone we left back in the twenty-sixth century to save *them*?" He pointed toward the Titanic.

She trembled in silence.

"They're already dead."

Her head drooped and she closed her eyes.

TC and Blake looked on, desperate to speak, yet with nothing to say.

Jennifer pulled free from Danny's weak grasp and leaned against the console, staring at the viewscreen. Together, they watched and waited.

TC was the first to break the silence. "How in the worlds did you convince Burnstone to let us target this point in time, Danny? He seemed pretty set on making sure we didn't get here until after the rescue ships were out of the area."

Danny started to open his mouth, but just dropped his head in silence.

"You didn't," Jennifer stated the obvious. "Did you?"

"Hey, if you're really worried, we could always stay back here in the twentieth century."

"Wonderful," TC sniped. "Life in the Stone Age."

"Industrial Age," Blake corrected.

"Figure of speech. Either way we're screwed."

Jennifer stood in front of Danny with her arms crossed. "And besides, what was the point of getting here *before* the crash? Wouldn't it have made more sense to show up a few days later? We can't contact the Silesians yet anyway. The only reason they're going to pay any attention to us is because we've got the package, and they won't need it until after the wreck."

"A lot can happen in a few days. I want to make sure we get to them right after they go down, send them home with as little information as possible."

"There!" Jennifer pointed to the main viewer. The inevitable collision had just occurred.

A chill swept across the deck of the Stargazer.

The *Titanic* continued on, veering slightly from its course. In the darkness, the infamous iceberg, briefly visible in the glow of the ship's lights, vanished from view within seconds.

"Enhancing," TC barked as he tapped a series of commands into his console. As the heat imaging scans were superimposed on the viewscreen, the luxury liner became bright red, and a distinct orange ball appeared, trailing away behind it."

Danny gave TC a slap on the back. "Nice work."

The distance between the two objects on screen continued to increase, then suddenly, the orange ball vanished.

"Blake," Danny barked, "get on those sensors. I want an exact location the minute those buggers hit bottom."

"On it," Blake said.

TC's attention was glued to the screen. The passenger ship was continuing on course. "They look OK," he said, more out of curiosity than relief. "Do you suppose…"

"They're taking on water." Blake squashed the glimmer of hope. "It's just a matter of time."

Jennifer looked away.

Danny walked up from behind and wrapped his arms around her.

The scene on the main viewer played out slowly, painfully as the four time travelers looked on. They could have zoomed in for a closer look, but no one really wanted to see the faces of history. They took turns sitting and pacing, but always watching as the minutes ticked by.

Off in the distance, a faint glimmer of light finally broke the monotony of the unchanging scene, as flares shot from the deck of the *Titanic* arced across the sky.

And still, the agony played on.

"I can't watch this anymore." Jennifer turned her head and went to Danny's quarters.

The next hour and a half was slow torture. Blake continued to monitor the course of the alien ship while Danny and TC pretended to make adjustments to the instruments on their consoles, but fleeting glimpses at the viewscreen captivated their attention.

Jennifer tossed and turned, periodically calling to the bridge for an update.

"Still nothing," Danny answered for the third time.

"How long has it been?"

"Just over an hour and a half since the flares."

"It's time." Jennifer headed back to the bridge. She didn't want to watch, but she couldn't *not* watch.

She entered the room, gaze fixed on the main viewer as the last of the ocean liner disappeared under the sea. She walked up beside her husband and took his hand. "All those people," she muttered beneath her breath, gaping at the scene as if she could see more than the dying light.

TC hung his head. "Rest their souls…again."

Danny turned to his partner, exhaling a deep breath through puffed cheeks. "Get to the shuttle bay. As soon as we've got a fix, I'm going to take the *Stargazer* down. We shouldn't have any trouble avoiding the life rafts out there, and nobody else is going to be around here for hours. I'll drop us to an altitude of fifteen hundred meters. You should be able to launch and have the shuttle under water within a couple of minutes."

"I'll be ready."

"Blake, you got a fix on those freaks? They must have hit bottom by now."

"Still tracking. They were holding their own for a while, but now they're sinking like a brick."

"Good. Once you've got the coordinates, get over to the shuttle and join TC. I want you aboard when it launches."

"Right. Man, look at them; that thing's all over the place. They're practically sitting in a centrifuge."

"Yeah, well let's not worry about them. We know *they* do OK."

Blake nodded. "Looks like they'll bottom out at least a mile from the Titanic."

"History already told us that."

"No," Blake corrected. "History *suggested* that. We didn't spot them until almost six centuries after the crash…they had plenty of time to relocate."

"I suppose," Danny said, "but there they are." He motioned toward the stationary blip on Blake's monitor.

"There they are," Blake agreed.

"Good. Get going."

Blake hurried off toward the shuttle bay.

"Take the nav, Jen." Danny sat back in his pilot seat. "Keep monitoring and let me know if there are any changes. I'm taking us in."

Jennifer sat down, eyes fixed on the scanner readout. The sphere lay motionless as Danny maneuvered the *Stargazer* directly above its position and well out of sight of the survivors clinging to lifeboats that floated slowly into the frigid night.

"We're in position, guys. Ready?"

TC watched Blake buckle in. "The hatch is sealed and we're secured for launch."

"Let's bump it, man."

"Not too much, I hope," TC muttered as he activated the outer doors of the launch bay.

With a tap on the nav panel, he triggered the electromagnetic drive and the shuttle lifted gracefully into the air. A short burst from the aft thrusters propelled them out from the protection of the Stargazer, but before gravity could take hold of the tiny craft, TC fired up the main engine and guided it safely toward the water. The Atlantic was relatively calm, but a small wave caught TC off-guard and jolted the shuttle as it entered the water. They listed sharply to the right, and an unmistakable thud came from the shuttle's small cargo hold, followed quickly by a faint "*umph*."

"Did you hear that?" TC asked.

"I heard something."

"Yeah. Must have been the probe smacking up against the side of the hull in the cargo hold."

"No way. I tied it down myself. That thing's tighter than a pilot's seat in an escape pod. Besides, metallic probes don't go '*umph*' when they hit something."

"You sure it was an '*umph*' and not a *thunk*."

"Definitely an '*umph*.'"

"Stowaway?"

"No one could've gotten through that security. A-17 is one of the tightest spots on the base."

"Got any other suggestions?" A look of horror swept over TC's face. "You don't think that dead Silesian we had in the Stargazer's cargo hold could have been pregnant, do you? What if something crawled out of it and slipped into the shuttle?"

"Nah. We'd have seen it when we loaded the probe."

"Did you check both cargo holds when you clamped the probe in?" TC looked toward the back of the ship, where two small cargo holds were sequestered behind the walls, one on either side.

Blake followed his gaze. "Didn't really see a need to."

"Still feel that way?"

"Look," Blake said, with a hint of hesitation, as if trying to convince himself, "that thing was dead for a long time. Even if it *was* pregnant, the baby...or babies, would have been dead too."

"You sure of that?"

"Pretty sure."

"And besides, what if it wasn't a baby? Maybe it was a parasite or something living inside of it, you know, like that old movie, *Alien*?"

"That crappy remake from my time?" Blake forced a laugh.

"Nah. The original."

"You gotta be kidding. You and Stryker must be the only two guys in the galaxy who still watch that old 2-D crap. What's with that?"

"Hey, they're classics, man. The actors are all real; none of that sim crap. Gritty stuff, and we've got the best collection in the Federation."

"That's because nobody else wants them."

"Maybe so, but..."

Blake reached for the controls of the shuttle and gave it a sharp jerk to the right.

Another dull thud echoed from the cargo area, this time followed by a short high-pitched squeal.

"OK, OK," TC said quietly. "So what now?"

Blake whispered back "You got any weapons on this thing?"

TC nodded and reached into a small panel in the front console, pulling out a phase pistol.

"Just one?" Blake rasped.

TC shrugged.

"Great, then you go check it out while I stay here and cower."

TC smiled nervously and inched his way back to the cargo area. The probe was secured in the bay on his left. He spread his feet to steady his stance and aimed the weapon toward the door on the right, then reached out with his left hand and tapped a panel on the adjacent wall. As the door slid up, there was another thud.

TC stumbled back, then thrust his weapon in the direction of the cargo bay.

The startled face of Margo Feldman poked out of the opening. "All right, all right!" she said, rubbing the back of her head. "Geez, I'd think you'd know how to fly this thing a little better, you being a Space Corps captain and all."

"God, lady!" TC yelped, still holding the charged pistol in her direction. "You scared the crap out of me."

"Eh-hemm," she said, motioning to the weapon. "Do you mind?"

TC stared at the gun in his hand, then sheepishly lowered it to his side and hit the button to power it down.

"Uh, sorry," he said.

"Margo?" Blake's voice rang out from the front of the vessel as he walked back to investigate.

"Hi, doc," she said, with an impish grin. "Does this mean I fail this semester?"

"How in the heck...? Didn't I leave you in charge of that Silesian specimen back in Omnicenter with specific instructions to stay out of trouble until I get back?"

"Give me a break, Dr. Richards. You didn't really think I was going to just hang out and watch that dead fish guy while all the action was out here, did you?"

"Well...yeah, actually. I did."

"Man, what century are you from? I mean, you may be incredibly cute, but you act like an old fart sometimes."

The two men looked at her, speechless.

Margo giggled nervously. "I didn't really say that out loud, did I?"

"Which part," TC chuckled, "the part where you called your professor a dork, or the part where you said you've got the hots for him?"

Margo lifted a hand to her forehead, shadowing a florid blush.

TC shook his head. "I'm going to get us back on course. You two work this out on your own." He turned and made his way back to the pilot's seat.

"Look, I don't have time for this right now," Blake snapped, "but it's not over by a long shot." He shook his head and sighed. "Now get back in there," he motioned into the cargo hold, "and strap yourself in."

"You're stashing me in the cargo hold? That's student abuse."

"You see any other seats around here?"

The entire shuttle could be viewed with one quick glance. Margo sighed and crawled back into the cargo compartment.

She looked up at Blake. "Can you at least get me a pillow or something?"

"Bottom panel," TC called back. The shuttle was too small to avoid inadvertent eavesdropping…not that TC was trying too hard to accomplish the task.

Blake opened the storage compartment in the back wall of the shuttle. Two small inflatable pillows were tucked in with other emergency supplies. He grabbed one and tossed it at Margo as he walked by. "You shouldn't have any trouble finding enough hot air to fill that thing," he sniped.

"Hey!" she called after Blake as he walked up front to join TC.

TC glanced over as Blake settled in next to him. "So, got your own little groupie, huh?"

Blake glared. "Let's just get this show on the road."

Chapter Twelve:
Apparition

TC piloted the shuttle toward the Silesian sphere, now marooned on the ocean floor. "So, you think they're really going to buy this?"

Blake shrugged. "Sure hope so."

"Why wouldn't they just assume we're hostile and blow us out of the water? I mean, if I were them, that's what I'd do."

"Good thing you're not them."

"Yeah."

The nav panel bleeped, and TC entered a minor course correction. "Should be there in a minute or so."

Blake nodded. "Look, if nothing else, once I start talking in Silesian it should at least buy us a little time while they try and figure out how much we know."

"You think they'll really believe we're from the future?"

"Doubt it. But hopefully, they'll be curious enough to take the probe in."

TC pointed to a flashing icon on the panel. "We're being scanned."

"Are they powering weapons?"

"Not that I can tell. Maybe their systems were damaged."

"Or maybe they figure we aren't worth the effort...yet."

"I like my idea better."

"Can you get us within fifty meters?"

"Why?"

"Just do it."

Blake donned a small wristband like the one Quigley was wearing when they'd met in the lab.

"Fifty meters."

"Warning," the ship's computer said. "Weapons targeting detected."

"Guess that answers one question," TC said. "Whatever you're going to do, I'd suggest you do it now."

"Right. Computer, monitor the audio patterns ten meters inside the hull of the sphere, shortest distance from this point. Amplify and play through this panel."

A dull hiss sounded from the comm panel.

Blake tapped a button on the wristband, projecting his image inside the sphere. There was no visual feedback, but he paused long enough so the appa-rition would be likely to draw attention. He then began clicking and squealing the prepared message.

TC winced and leaned back into his chair; within a few minutes, Blake was done, and they waited for the response.

"Weapons disengaged," the computer announced.

TC curled his mouth in admiration. "Not bad."

As Blake turned to him with a smile, the comm came alive with the now characteristic cacophony of the Silesian language. TC reached out and tapped down the volume. "Doesn't really help all that much, does it?" he muttered.

Blake ignored him and answered the aliens.

"That it?" TC asked when the noise stopped.

Blake nodded. "They are ready to accept the probe."

"Send it out."

Blake went back to the cargo area and moved the probe into the decompression chamber located under the floor. Although designed primarily to provide access to outer space, the chamber was also equipped to equalize pressure under water. Blake climbed out and sealed the hatch.

"All set," he called to TC.

"Right. Flooding the chamber." TC tapped a sequence into the panel on the command console, opening a valve adjacent to the outer decompression chamber door, and water began to rush in.

Blake took a seat beside TC and they watched the indicator on the command panel as the chamber filled.

"Chamber pressure equalized," the ship's computer announced as the last bit of air was replaced with seawater.

TC tapped in another sequence to open the outer door.

"Voice confirmation required," the computer said.

"Open outer cargo air-lock door," TC said.

"Confirmed," the computer responded. "Opening outer cargo air-lock door."

TC guided the probe out of the cargo hold with a mechanical arm as he and Blake watched its progress on the monitor. Once clear of the shuttle's hull, TC released the clamps, and the probe floated away slowly.

"She's clear," Blake said.

TC nodded and triggered the maneuvering engine on the probe, sending it in the direction of the Silesian sphere.

Margo had crept up behind them. "Cool."

"Blake!" TC snapped.

"Margo!" Blake glared over his shoulder. "Didn't I tell you to stay put?"

"You didn't really expect me to just lay there while all this was going on. Did you?"

The side of Blake's mouth curled. "Yes?"

"Phsh!" She rolled her eyes. "Get real, doc."

"Look!" TC pointed at his monitor.

They all looked to the viewscreen as a green light shot out from the sphere and encompassed the probe, pulling it inside.

"*Major* cool," Margo whispered.

"Yeah," TC muttered. "Major cool."

Blake activated the comm and asked the Silesians if the transfer was successful. They indicated it was, and that they should be ready for take-off within the hour.

"I'd suggest we vacate the area," he said, explaining his conversation to TC and Margo. "We have no idea what effect their engines may have on our shuttle, and I don't think we want to find out."

"Agreed," TC said. "I'd feel better watching this from the Stargazer."

"Margo," Blake said with authority, pointing back toward the cargo bay.

"All right, all right. But just til we're airborne."

"You stay put until we're back on the ship, young lady," TC snapped, "or you're gonna get to experience some artificial sleep." He pointed to his hand phaser. Even on the low setting, it packed enough of a wallop to knock her out cold for hours.

"You wouldn't dare!"

"Don't try me, kid."

"Dr. Richards?" she pleaded. "You wouldn't really let him do that, would you?"

"Hey, he's the captain."

Margo looked horrified and slinked back to the cargo bay to secure herself in.

TC watched, then turned and smiled. "You know I wouldn't have really done it."

Blake returned the look. "You know I wouldn't have let you."

*

The shuttle popped up out of the water and made its way back to the Stargazer, gliding easily into the shuttle bay. The two men, feeling just a bit guilty, helped Margo out of the cargo hold and accompanied her to the bridge.

"Where in God's name did *she* come from?" Danny asked as they walked in.

"Seems we had a stow-away," TC said.

"You are in deep trouble, young lady."

"*Margo*," she hissed through clenched teeth.

"Excuse me?"

"My name is Margo, not *young lady*, so everybody just stop calling me that." She her wrenched her arm away from TC.

The side of TC's mouth curled up. "Oh, I can think of a few other things to call you."

"Later, kids," Blake pointed to the main viewscreen.

The Silesians had maneuvered their sphere hundreds of miles away from the site of the *Titanic* to avoid being spotted as they emerged from the water. Blake had tracked their movement and brought the *Stargazer* to within twenty miles of the iridescent sphere as it broke the plane of the ocean and began to lift gracefully into the sky. Within seconds, the technological marvel was accelerating towards space when it suddenly burst into a fiery ball.

Five pairs of hands shot up instinctively against the brilliant flash of light.

"Whoa," Margo said. "I'll bet *that* wasn't part of the plan."

TC peered at her. "What did you do to that probe?"

"*Me*? Why would I have messed with it?"

TC tipped his head toward the screen, still bright with the afterglow of the explosion.

"What, are you kidding?" Margo rasped. "I risked my neck just for a chance to come out here and see one of them."

"So you say."

"Besides, even if I wanted to sabotage them for some bizarre reason, how would I know what to do? Do I look like a quantum physicist?"

"You don't need to be a quantum physicist to plant a malicious virus. Hell, even if you were just over-exercising your annoyingly inquisitive little brain, you could have screwed it up by accident."

"Look you..." Margo's face was turning red as she prepared to lunge at the athletic TC McGee, easily twice her size.

"All right, all right," Danny said. "Let's all just calm down, shall we?"

"Right," TC said. "I mean, we're standing in a time machine, right? We can fix this."

"Ah, hell," Danny muttered with a wave of the hand. "What's the difference? They're gone, right?"

Jennifer looked horrified. "You have *got* to be kidding! All those lives..." her voice trailed off and she stood in silence.

"Hey. *We* didn't blow them up," Danny said.

TC fixed his gaze on Margo.

"Oh, gimme a break!" she snapped, and then plopped down into one of the chairs.

Danny glanced in her direction, then back at TC. "Come on. I don't believe for one minute this girl had anything to do with that blast."

"*Thank* you." Margo glared at TC.

"And you don't either, TC," Danny continued.

TC shrugged.

"That repair kit was put together by the guys in the giant fish ball from the future," Danny said. "Obviously, they didn't want anybody from the past coming back to haunt them."

"Of course," Jennifer nodded. "It makes perfect sense. They didn't want these things in their future any more than we wanted them in our past. They never even knew there were Silesian survivors here, and now, with this explosion…there weren't."

"Yeah," Margo said, eyes widening. "There won't be a trace of their existence here other than what the four of us know. When we get back to the future, the sphere will be gone. As a matter of fact, it will never have been there in the first place, because they won't ever get that distress call. There won't be any confrontation with Earth and no reason for anyone else to even know they exist."

"And our mission will have been a success," Danny said. "No weird aliens to deal with, no nuclear explosion ripping up the ocean floor."

"But to kill all of those people…" Jennifer still could not believe that any advanced culture could be so cavalier about the mass killing of their own kind.

"It *is* pretty sick," Blake agreed. "But what can we do about it? If we try to go back and correct the problem, we have no way of making sure their repairs will go any better the next time around. In fact, we could make things a lot worse if these aliens not only survive, but survive with the knowledge that they're being hunted down."

"Right," Danny agreed. "Let's leave well enough alone and get the hell out of here.

"Sorry, kid," TC said to Margo.

"Thanks," she said.

"No, I mean…*sorry*," he repeated, motioning to the navigation chair that Margo had settled into. "I need you out of my chair."

Margo rolled her eyes and heaved a sigh as she got up. "And I suppose you want me strapped into that little cargo hold on the shuttle again?"

"Hey, it was good enough for you when you decided to stow away."

"TC!" Jennifer scolded.

"Just kidding, doc," he smiled.

Jennifer motioned to Margo. "Come on. Let's go calculate the jump."

Chapter Thirteen:
The Dome of Science

It didn't take long for Jennifer to calculate the jump sequence, sending them back to the future, arriving just minutes after their original departure. They were still recovering as they approached Omnicenter.

Danny was the first to notice it.

"Do you guys see that?" he asked, peering at the viewscreen.

Blake and TC looked up from the navigation and communication displays they had been concentrating on. The ship was approaching Omnicenter, and the city was just coming into focus, growing progressively larger on the screen. The metallic sheen of its over-developed architecture cast a bright reflection that obscured many of the city's details.

"Yeah," TC said. "Butt-ugly as ever."

"I don't know…" Danny's voice trailed off. "Something just doesn't look right."

Blake walked up behind Danny, peering over his shoulder. "That's odd."

"What?" Jennifer's voice came over the intercom. She had been watching on the small monitor screen in Danny's quarters. "All I see is a bright dot on this thing. What are you guys looking at."

"The reflection from the buildings," Blake said. "Look at the pattern of the light. It's not dissipating away from the structures like you'd expect. It's focusing in a sort of…"

"Dome!" Danny was the first to realize the change in a sight indelibly etched in his pilot's mind. "What the hell is that?"

TC swung his chair around. "On it." He began to scan the dome. "Some sort of energy shield."

The shape was getting brighter as they approached, gradually morphing into a hemisphere of light surrounding the entire city.

"Whoa, cool," Margo rasped. She and Jennifer had just come onto the bridge to see what all the fuss was about.

Danny slowed their approach. "How's it coming, TC?"

"We'll never get through that without shields, but it's modulating. It'll take a few cycles to set the parameters."

"How long?"

"Depends on the duration of each cycle."

Danny reset the landing sequence to put them in a holding pattern when they approached to a thousand meters.

"We're being hailed," the computer announced.

Stryker nodded. "On my monitor."

"Stargazer, do you read?"

Danny fumbled for the controls while still focused on the forward viewer. "Uh, yeah, Omnicenter. Loud and clear. What the heck's going on down there?"

"I was just going to ask you the same thing, sir. Why aren't your shields up?"

Danny glanced at TC, who waved him off.

He looked back at the screen. "What the hell is that thing?"

"*What* thing, sir?"

"What thing? That humongous energy field hanging over your head."

There was a brief pause on the other end, then – "Uh, Stargazer, break off your approach and back off to three thousand meters. We'll send someone to escort you in."

Stryker looked down at his monitor, a blue screen with the Space Corps logo. "Who is this?"

The pause was deafening.

"This is Captain Stryker. Identify yourself."

"Lieutenant Griggs, sir. I suggest you halt your approach immediately. If you don't burn up in the dome, you'll be shot down."

"Shot down!" Danny yelled at a blank screen. "Dammit, where the hell's your video?"

"Standard protocol, sir. Is this some kind of test?"

"Just patch me through to Kolanski's office, would you?"

"No need, Danny." It was Ski's voice. The viewscreen lit up with his face."

"Ski, nice to see a friendly face. What the hell's going on down there?"

"What do you mean? Did TC put you up to this, man? Why are you giving my guys such a hard time? I know you two are pranksters, but this is a bit much even for you, isn't it? A few more seconds and you'd have been toast. Even *your* ship can't get her shields up that fast."

"Our shields are off-line, Ski," Jennifer said.

"Well," a grin spread across Kolanski's face, "Jennifer, it's good to see you. I thought Danny was still keeping you locked away in that android shop of yours."

TC glanced over at Danny with a puzzled look. Kolanski had just talked to Jennifer that morning.

"Yeah, well I'm here now." She raised an eyebrow. "And *no one* keeps me locked away."

Danny swore he could see Ski blush.

"Uh...yeah, sorry, Jen," he stammered. "Just an expression, you know?"

Jennifer laughed. "It's good to see you too. Now can you send up a ship to take us through? We need to come in for repairs."

Ski turned away from the monitor. "Hmm?"

A vague murmur came through the Stargazer's comm system, someone talking to Kolanski in the background.

"Lieutenant Griggs here says our scans don't show any damage to your shields."

"Lieutenant Griggs is wrong," Jennifer said authoritatively. "Our generators are intact, but the software we need to calculate the shield frequency crashed."

"Whatever," TC said. "In either case, we can't get through without an escort. You going to let us in today, man?"

Kolanski laughed. "Help's on the way. I'll see you when you get down."

The transmission cut off.

"Interesting," Blake said.

Danny frowned. "More like confusing. What the hell is going on here?"

"We obviously disrupted the timeline," Blake said. Something we did back in the twentieth century changed the future."

"Impossible," Danny said. "All we did was get rid of the Silesians, and they were in hiding; nobody ever even knew they were there."

"Maybe not. But they obviously affected the timeline. We didn't interact with anything else."

"We need to get back and fix this," Jennifer said.

"Fix, what?" Danny asked. "We don't even know what's happened in the past five centuries. Hell, maybe we made things better. I mean, that was the point, wasn't it?"

"Well, yeah, but…"

"We can argue about this later, guys," TC said. "We've got company."

Three small starfighters were streaking towards them.

"Whatever happens," Blake said, "I suggest we stick to the faulty software story and tell them we've just come from Kennedy Prime for a visit. Agreed?"

Everyone nodded.

"Stargazer?" the squadron leader queried.

"Yes?"

"Stay in our center until we reach the spaceport. We'll take you through the shield, then stay with us until you land in A-13."

"Copy that," Danny replied. He knew they would have plenty of company when they landed.

The squadron formed a triangle around the Stargazer, and then activated an energy shield around the entire formation. Stryker kept his ship dead center. They penetrated the dome without incident, and were docked at Omnicenter Spaceport within minutes.

The squadron had escorted them to the spaceport's Section A, the same high security area from which they had departed. A-13 was reserved for suspicious visitors who were considered a potential threat. With walls reinforced by a vitanium honeycomb infrastructure, it was impenetrable by any known hand weapon, and difficult to breach even from close range with standard starfighter weapons. Once inside, the shock wave from any blast strong enough to penetrate the walls of Bay A-13 would also destroy whoever was bold enough…or stupid enough…to fire the shot in the first place.

"Guess they don't trust us, huh?" TC said.

"Apparently not," Danny muttered.

The ship eased into the landing bay, and the roof slid shut overhead. As the crew filed out, they were greeted by a heavily armed contingent. One of the guards scanned them for weapons, then turned and gave the all clear.

As Kolanski entered the room, he paused and looked his old friends over closely. It wasn't unheard of for pirates to commandeer a ship, and then try to gain entry to secure areas by using holomitter rings to help them masquerade as the real crew.

"What's happening, Ski?" Danny greeted him with a smile. "All this just for us?" He motioned around the room.

Kolanski approached slowly, then reached out and poked at Danny's chest, looking for the characteristic shimmer of a holoemitter. "Hmph."

"What? You don't believe it's us?"

"I don't know what to think. I mean, what was that with the shields? Even if they were on the fritz, you know better than to try and fly through the dome without them. Besides," he said, looking over at Blake Richards and Margo Feldman, "The Stryker and McGee I know would never let civilians set foot on their ship."

"Yeah," TC said glaring at Margo, who unabashedly returned the look, "well, we didn't figure on a stowaway."

Margo sneered.

As Danny turned back toward Kolanski, he noticed several pinpoints of bright green light dancing across his chest, the familiar targeting lasers of standard issue pulse rifles.

"Come on, guys. All those years of training and this is the best you can do?" He motioned to his shirt. "How about a dancing bear or something."

Ski tried hard to bite back the smile that forced its way through his terse military demeanor, but lost in the end. "God, it's got to be you, Stryker."

"Look, Ski," Danny said. "I really think we'd better take this someplace private."

"Look around you. There's no more secure place on the planet."

Danny looked at all of the armed men standing around, weapons still trained on his make-shift crew. "No. I mean *for your ears only* kind of private."

Ski studied Danny's face.

"Look," Danny said, "escort us wherever you want and with all the guards you've got, but when we talk, make sure it's just you and me in that room. Believe me, you'll thank me when you hear what I've got to say."

They were escorted to a private security room just inside the space-port. TC was instructed to wait outside, along with Margo, Blake and Jennifer, in the company of a small contingency of guards. Kolanski entered the room with Danny and sat facing him across a small polished steel table. Danny looked up at the security cameras without saying a word.

"Video only," Kolanski ordered to his unseen men. He looked over at Danny. "Well. What's so damned secret you couldn't tell me out there."

Danny took in a deep breath, then puffed his cheeks and let the air out slowly. "There's a simple explanation why all this doesn't make sense, why we seem out of place here."

"I'm listening." Ski eased back in his chair.

"Well, actually, we're not out of place, we're…" Danny hesitated and cleared his throat. "We're out of time."

"Time for what?" Ski asked. "What have the Neanders cooked up now? Have they launched another invasion?"

"No, no," Danny said. "I mean…not that I know of…I doubt it."

"Oh, well that clears things up."

"What I mean," Danny said slowly, enunciating each word, "is that we're out of *our* time, out of the normal space-time continuum. We're not from this timeline."

Ski stared in disbelief. "Oh, come on, Danny. Not this again. I know you've been obsessed with time travel ever since you went back to the Old West, but you know as well as I do that all that technology was destroyed. Even Jennifer couldn't get her hands on everything she'd need to put a time-warp system together."

"Yeah, well in our timeline, she could. And what's more, it was sanctioned by you."

"No way."

"Yeah…way. You and Stoney."

"There is no way you could've talked Burnstone into this."

"I didn't have to. Heck, it was his idea."

"Come on, I don't buy that for a minute. Congress has strictly forbidden time travel, and Burnstone is always by the book. You don't get to be general if you're not."

"You also don't get to be general unless you know when the book needs a little editing. It was either sanction time travel or face certain destruction by a hostile alien force. There was no time to wait for a decision from Congress. There was really only one choice to make, and he made it."

Ski opened his mouth, but didn't know how to respond.

"Look, Ski. Just hear me out. When we're done, I'll take you down to the *Stargazer* to see the time-warp generator for yourself."

Kolansi studied Danny's face. "All right. Let's hear it."

Danny proceeded to explain the whole sequence of events, right up to the time they spotted the dome. When he was done, Kolanski sat back and crossed his legs, then looked into Danny's eyes.

"You're serious?"

"Dead serious."

"So what, are you expecting a medal or something?"

"Hardly. We obviously screwed something up. Are you expecting an attack?"

"Attack?" For a brief moment, Ski looked puzzled, then enlightenment swept across his face. "Ah...the domes. Nah, they might provide a little deterrent, but nothing we'd need as long as the defense system's working. They're to keep out the radiation."

"What radiation?"

"From the sun. What? You guys don't have that problem?"

"What happened to your sun?"

"It's not the sun, it's the ozone layer."

"OK. So what happened to it."

"Pollution. Greenhouse gases. We didn't realize it until global warming started in the twenty-third century, and by then it was too late to reverse the effect."

"Twenty-third century! Hell, we figured it out in the twentieth. Even the cretins back then knew it was from air pollution. Where I come from, the ozone layer is just fine. We don't need any shields."

"Well, *we* sure as hell do. What the hell did you guys do back there?"

"Just our mission. It doesn't make any sense."

They sat silently for a few minutes, then Ski threw his hands up. "I'm going to go get Jennifer. Maybe she can shed some light on this."

The metal chair screeched against the floor as Kolanski stood. He walked out of the room and returned a few seconds later with Jennifer and Blake.

Danny looked up and Kolanski motioned to Blake. "Jennifer insisted," he said.

"So," Jennifer glanced at Ski and then back to Danny, "you two just catching up on old times, or what?"

"Oh yeah," Danny said. "Just shooting the breeze."

Ski motioned to the chairs around the table and everyone sat.

"So, where are we at?"

"Danny told me how you saved the world," Ski said.

"And Ski told *me* what we screwed up," Danny said. "We just can't figure out how." He filled her in on what Kolanski had said.

Jennifer shook her head. "It must have been something the aliens did after the crash, something we never knew about. But even if we figure it out, we might just screw things up more if we try to go back and fix it."

"Oh well, at least you've got the domes, right?" Danny said to Kolanski.

"Yeah, well let's just forget for a minute how incredibly stupid that sounds. Even if that were a remotely acceptable alternative to saving the atmosphere, it's still not enough. See, the part I didn't tell you is that it's getting worse. Even with the domes, Earth will be uninhabitable in a few more decades. In fact, we've already started evacuating to the outworlds. This will be a dead planet in forty years."

"Kind of an important little fact to have left out, don't you think?" Danny muttered.

"Yeah, well, there it is."

"My God," Jennifer said. "How could getting rid of the Silesians have had that much of an effect here? All they were doing was hiding on the bottom of the ocean the whole time. Besides, global warming was so obvious – the icecaps were melting, glaciers were vanishing, temperatures were warming all over the globe. It's not like we needed somebody to help us figure it out. How could it have taken you so long?"

Blake's eyes widened. "Maybe we did."

"Did what?"

"Need help figuring it out."

"What do you mean?"

"The Zone f the Tenth Degree."

"Zone of the Tenth Degree?" Kolanski was lost.

"Don't get him started," Danny said.

"It doesn't matter anyway," Blake said. "At least not the details. What it boils down to is that the Silesian colony produced a lot of heat, and I mean a *lot*, enough to accelerate the global warming that was just starting to occur from events taking place on the surface."

"Of course," Jennifer said, following Blake's line of reasoning. "And that rapid change in climate is what caught people's attention. They discovered the damage pollution was doing and were able to stop it before it was too late."

"Something we never had a shot at here," Ski added. "By the time *our* glaciers started to disappear, the ozone layer was irreparably damaged."

"So," TC said, "in order to save Earth from destruction, we've got to go back and undo what we did."

"And then we're back to square one," Danny said. "Assuming we even *can* go back and undo what we did, we'd still have a giant sphere ready to blow us all to hell when we get back to *our* twenty-sixth century. Which ending for Earth would you prefer?"

Danny looked Steven Kolanski square in the eye. "Look, there's really only one option here."

"You always see things as black or white, don't you, Danny?"

"Well, yeah, when they're painted that way."

"And just which way is that?"

"You got to let us go back and fix this thing – undo what we did in the twentieth century."

Ski glared at Danny. "Now let me get this straight. You're telling me the only reason we've got the ozone problem is because you exiled some alien race that inhabited the Atlantic Ocean back in the 1900's, right?"

"Uh huh."

"And so if I send you back to restore the original timeline, all of this will have never happened."

"Right," Danny said with a smile. "Simple, huh?"

"Yeah. Simple. All I have to do is send you back and you'll make all of this disappear. Everything I know, my whole life." He snapped his fingers. "Just like that."

Danny shrugged sheepishly. "Guess it doesn't sound so good when you put it that way."

"Nope, not so much."

"Look, Ski," Jennifer interrupted. "You can't think of it like that. You're in the other timeline too, the one we came from. The Earth in this timeline is about to become uninhabitable anyway. We wouldn't be destroying *your* timeline, we'd be saving *our* timeline," she motioned back and forth. "Yours included – your *other* timeline."

"So you say. But the bottom line is that everything I've ever known will be gone."

"No it won't. It'll just be different, better. You, and everyone else here, will be able to stay on Earth."

Ski sighed as his gaze dropped to the floor. "I don't know…" He turned to Danny. "And you're sure you can do this? You can just go back and undo what you did?"

"Piece of cake," Danny said, slapping him on the shoulder.

"Don't suppose I can go with you?"

Jennifer rubbed his arm gently. "You're already there."

*

Kolanski accompanied his three friends, along with Margo Feldman, back to Bay A-13, where the *Stargazer* sat untouched by the Space Corps guards assigned to watch it. Jennifer led him into the ship and back to engineering, where the time-warp generator sat quiescently.

"My God," he whispered. "I never realized how small it was."

"Quigley never let you near the prototype, huh?"

"Not even in the same room," he smiled. "Who'd have guessed that something so small could change history."

"Want to know how it works?" Jennifer asked.

"Nah. I'd never follow all the geek speak anyhow. It's enough just to know that it does."

She walked him out of engineering.

"You won't regret this, man," TC said as he watched Kolanski disembark.

"I already do." Ski walked down the ramp. "Open launch doors."

"Yes, sir." The guard on duty turned and tapped the authorization code into the security panel.

As the ceiling doors of Bay A-13 parted, the *Stargazer* rose gracefully out into the daylight, glistening in silence. Kolanski looked on introspectively and braced for the characteristic thruster burst that would send his friends darting back into space, leaving him wondering if he would feel anything, if he would ever know what had happened once they reshaped history.

*

"Good job, Ace," TC said. "I thought for a while there that we were going to be living in the Space Corps brig.

"The only question now," Danny asked, "is where do we go and what do we do?"

"Maybe," TC slowly thought out loud, "we could go back to the twentieth century some time after that sphere blew up and do something to help them figure out the whole global warming thing."

"And this from the guy who doesn't like to time travel." Jennifer quipped.

TC shrugged.

"Too risky," Blake said.

Margo sighed audibly. "Well, it's better than ending up right back here in dome-world again."

TC glared. "When we need your help, we'll ask for it."

Margo glared right back. "Hey, I'm agreeing with you here."

"Nah, Danny said, "Blake's right. But we can't just do nothing."

"Then what?" TC asked.

"I believe I may have the answer," Blake said.

Chapter Fourteen:
Diplopia

One hour before the crash of the Titanic

The *Stargazer* appeared in the night sky over the icy Atlantic waters one hundred meters from their prior point of entry.

Blake looked up as Jennifer walked onto the bridge.

"So, how're we doing?" she asked.

"Perfect jump, but it won't be long before the other *Stargazer* gets here. We should put some distance between us before they drop out of time-warp."

"Yeah," Danny agreed. "Let's not spook them till we have to."

TC shook his head. "This is weird, man."

"Tell me about it."

Danny piloted the *Stargazer* several hundred miles out.

"We'll wait here and contact them over subspace when they pop in."

Margo was transfixed on the main viewer. "This should be interesting."

"For once," TC said without looking up, "I agree with you."

She glanced his way and allowed a barely perceptible smile to creep across her face.

"There," Jennifer said, pointing to a small flicker of light. "That's the energy surge of a time-warp."

TC looked down at the scanners and tapped on the control panel. "Sensor confirmation. That's her."

"*Very* cool," Margo whispered.

"Computer," Danny said.

"Yes, Captain?"

"Open a channel. Standard Space Corps frequency, and encode it with encryption Zeta 4. Audio only."

"Affirmative."

Danny and TC had devised the Zeta 4 code themselves, and only used it for messages between each other. For his counterpart on the other ship, there wouldn't be any mistaking the source.

"Stargazer, do you read?"

The familiar voice that came back through the comm was uncharacteristically tentative. "*Stargazer* here. Who the hell is this and why aren't you sending video?"

"Yeah…," Danny sputtered, "about that."

"Look, light it up or this conversation's over."

"Hey, I'll show you mine if you show me yours."

"You first. *You* contacted *me*, remember?"

"All right, but brace yourself."

Danny motioned to TC, who activated video, and the startled look of Danny's mirror image stared back from the main viewer.

"Who the hell *are* you?" he barked. "You steal my encryption code, you steal my face, and then you've got the nerve to hail me? Turn that damn holoemitter off and let me see your face."

He looked off screen, and they could hear TC's voice. "Can't pinpoint it, Ace. They're not showing on our scanners."

It wasn't too hard for TC to fool the sensors of the duplicate ship; nobody knew her better.

The Stryker on screen was fuming. "Where the hell are you and why are you hiding from us?"

Danny shook his head. "In a minute, but first…" he turned to Jennifer. "Look, could you cover your ears for a sec?"

"What!" she snapped. "You have *got* to be kidding. If you really think…"

"Hey!" Danny interrupted, gazing directly into her eyes with an intensity that touched her soul. "Trust me, would you?"

Jennifer reluctantly put her hands up to her ears.

"Thanks," Danny said, and then turned back to the viewscreen.

"Listen, Stryker. Last week, remember picking up that diamond for your anniversary?"

The face on the screen contorted with confusion. "Yeah? What of it? Anybody could've seen me buy that."

"But nobody saw you when you melted the gold for the setting back home in the basement." He glanced over at Jen, standing dutifully with her hands over her ears. Then, turning back to the viewscreen, he continued in a loud whisper. "You molded it into an arch, just like the one on Eden over Le Lac D'Amour where you married Jen."

The Stryker on screen looked dumbfounded. Danny knew no one else could have known about that. He was alone that night, and he hadn't even told TC about it.

"You see, old friend," he continued, "I know about that because I did it. I *am* you. I'm from your future."

"Now wait a minute," the screen face said. "We just got back here to the past. Why in the worlds would you be looking for me here?"

"It's a long story."

"Then why don't you shuttle on over here," he sneered. "We'll talk about it over a drink. I'd love to meet myself."

Danny returned the sneer.

TC reached over to Jennifer and gently pulled her hands away from her ears.

"Well?" she whispered to him. "What'd I miss?"

"Can't tell you," he whispered back, "but he had a good reason."

"Eh-hmm!" Danny cleared his voice, raising an eyebrow in their direction.

TC motioned as if to say *sorry*.

Danny turned back to the viewscreen. "Well, as much as I'd love to see you…or see me…or…whatever, we don't have time to socialize. Just listen up; we've already been through what you are about to do, and the mission goes great; everything works fine. The Silesians take the probe – by the way that reminds me, you've got a stowaway in the shuttle's cargo hold…"

"Hey!" Margo protested.

"Well, you were!"

She folded her arms across her chest defiantly, and Danny turned back to the screen.

"She's harmless," he said, "just a little too curious for her own good. Let Blake take care of her. He'll know what to do.

"Anyhow, the fish people take the probe. It works just fine until they get the ship into space, and then it blew them all to hell; lit up the whole sky."

The Stryker on screen shrugged his shoulders. "And the problem with that is?"

"I know, I know. It didn't sound so bad to me either, but somehow it screws up the future."

The alternate Stryker looked dubious. "So let me get this straight. We get rid of a bunch of freeloaders who nobody ever even knew existed, and it still mucks things up?"

"Right," Danny said.

"And this is supposed to make sense how?"

Blake tapped Danny on the shoulder. "If I may?"

The alternate Stryker glanced over his shoulder at the alternate Blake Richards on his own bridge, then back towards the screen. "This is too weird, man."

"Look ," Blake said to the viewscreen, "it all makes perfect sense really. You see…"

"The short version," the alternate Stryker on the screen said impatiently.

Danny smiled. "Some things are the same in every timeline."

Blake cleared his throat loudly. "As I was saying…the Silesians didn't blow up their colonists to protect our timeline, they did it for themselves."

The Stryker on the screen nodded. "No big surprise there, but how does that screw up *our* future?"

"Short version," Danny whispered to Blake.

Blake shook his head. "Great. Stereo," he muttered, and went on to explain what they'd found in the future.

"Quite a fish tale, Blake."

Danny burst out laughing.

The Stryker on the screen smiled back. "I'm glad someone shares my sense of humor."

Jennifer shook her head. "This is *so* pathetic."

"It makes sense actually," came a muted voice behind the Stryker on screen.

"What does?" Jennifer asked.

"Blake's explanation," the voice sounded back.

"Sounds like my Blake agrees with you," the alternate Stryker said.

Danny huffed. "What a surprise."

The screen Stryker smiled. "So do I, actually. But what do we do? If we just do nothing and go back to the future, that damn alien warship will still be hovering over the Atlantic when we get there."

"Precisely," Blake said, "which is why we'll have to convince them that we're too dangerous to mess with; that we really did go back in time, figure out their plan, and refuse to play along; that we could just as easily go back and set off a nuke to blow their mothership up at the precise moment it arrived here."

"And just how do you propose we do that?" the alternate Stryker asked. "They're not exactly intimidated by us and we don't have any proof we can do all that."

"It won't be easy, but I've got a pretty good idea how to make them listen."

The face on the screen smiled back. "I thought you might."

"One little problem, though," Blake added. "We can't both go back."

The crew of both ships knew what he meant immediately. They had all studied time travel theory, and the basic thinking was that if two versions of the same person were to exist at the same time, then the space-time continuum could be destabilized.

"God," muttered TC, "I hadn't thought about that."

"Well, didn't we just prove that wrong?" Margo asked. "I mean, here we are now, both of us, and nothing's happening."

"Nothing we can perceive yet," Blake said, "but the longer we interact with this timeline, the more likely it is that our actions will contradict each other – the same person doing two different things at the same time – it'll be pulling the timeline in two different directions simultaneously. Only one *Stargazer* can go back to the twenty-sixth century. Only one crew can return home."

"And which one would that be," the alternate Stryker asked hesitantly.

"I'm afraid that has to be you and your crew," Danny said to his alternate self.

"What!" Margo shrieked from behind him. "But *we* know more than they do. *We* were the ones who poked around inside that sphere under the Atlantic, *we* were the ones who went to the other future and back, and *our* Blake's the one with the plan for how to deal with the aliens once we get back home."

"Yeah," Danny said somberly, "but we may not be able to get back. See, if we try to go back to the future now, we'll go right back to where we just came from, back to the alternate future and the Dome of Doom. And if we sit here and wait until after the time we blew up that sphere, to try and get back to our original timeline, then the mission we went on, all our actions after we engaged the sphere, will have never happened. The timeline that we have been traveling will have never happened. And we…"

"Will cease to exist," TC completed the thought in a near whisper. "Change a sentinel event in a timeline and that timeline, along with everything and everybody in it, will cease to exist," he quoted from Daystrom's classic article.

"Bingo," Danny said.

"But that's not possible," Margo said desperately, facing her own mortality. "Is it? It can't be possible."

"Hang on a minute, guys," Jennifer waved a finger. "We proved that theory wrong when we blew up the alien sphere; we changed our own timeline, the one we came from, and we're still here."

"Absolutely right," Blake said. "Apparently, as long as you're in the new timeline before the old one is obliterated, you're OK. After all, we *didn't* vanish when we changed our original timeline, now did we? We traveled into the new future unharmed."

"Then I agree with Margo," the alternate Stryker said from the viewscreen. *Your* crew has to be the one to make the trip. The stuff you learned when you blew up the first sphere could give you the edge you need to defeat the other one, the one hanging over the Atlantic in 2503. You've got a better shot at them than we do."

"And what about you?" Danny asked.

"We jump into 2600. I figure by then, you'll all be dead and gone, except maybe Blake."

Margo's face lit up. "Why Blake?"

"Shh," Blake put up a hand.

"But…"

"Later," he snapped, then turned to the screen. "Go on, Danny."

The Stryker on screen dipped his head apologetically. "Right. Well, when we get there, we check the history records. If your mission failed, then we go back to 2503 and try to take out the sphere ourselves. If your mission succeeded, then we take on new identities and start out fresh in the twenty-seventh century."

"I like the way this guy thinks," Danny said of his alternate self.

Both Jennifers rolled their eyes.

"This whole thing's too Sartre for me," Margo said.

"Yeah," TC muttered, "I think, therefore I am…I think."

"That wasn't Sartre," Margo said."

"You sure? I could have sworn…"

"Whatever," Danny snapped. He looked at his alternate self on the viewscreen. "Look, you're going to have to know our plan in case we fail so you don't screw up the same way when it's your turn. We've got seventeen minutes to brief you guys on what we've been through and on Blake's plan for dealing with that big tank of fish when we get back to the twenty-sixth century.

"Blake," he said, pulling Blake out of earshot from Margo. "Uplink with the other Blake. Give him all our mission details and brief him on your plan."

Blake nodded and walked back to the comm station. Danny motioned for Jennifer to distract Margo. If they did somehow survive this, it would be better to have her know as little as possible about Blake. She understood and led Margo back to Danny's quarters.

It took just ten minutes for the Blakes to exchange information. When the download was complete, the alternate Blake Richards signalled his captain.

"Got it, fellas," the alternate Stryker said. "Time for you to get going. No point tempting fate by having both of us hanging around here."

"Right," Danny said. "Get ready to bump it, gang."

"Not just yet," Blake said. "If we jump now, we'll probably jump back to the alternate future we just came from. We need to wait until after the time-line was originally changed – after we blew up the sphere – and then make the jump to 2503."

"OK," Danny said, "but I want to be ready to jump as soon as we pass the change point."

Jennifer and Margo settled into Danny's tight quarters, where Jennifer got to work on the calculations for the jump back to 2503. TC anxiously paced the metal floors of the bridge and Danny sat silently as Blake monitored the clock, watching the critical seconds tick away.

"That's it," he said, breaking the silence. "Time zero has passed."

"Finally." Danny wiped a bead of sweat off his brow. "Let's get out of here."

His counterpart stood stoically in the center of the group on the other side of the viewscreen. "Take care of my world."

Danny nodded through a forced smile before turning away.

"Engage."

Chapter Fifteen:
World's Biggest Golf Ball

The *Stargazer* re-entered the twenty-sixth century over the Pacific Ocean due east of Pearl Harbor at eight PM local time. The verdant volcanic peaks of the Hawaiian Islands jutting sharply out of the deep blue waters of the Pacific were silhouetted by a brilliant orange flame of light, the last rays of departing sun.

Jennifer gazed longingly into the distance. "I'd forgotten how beautiful it is here."

The softness of her voice broke Danny's concentration. He glanced back over his shoulder at Jennifer and followed her gaze toward the scene playing out on the forward viewer. His tension melted away with a sigh. "Maybe after we get done…" his voiced trailed off. "That is, if any of this is still here."

His words of desperation spoiled the mood, and Jennifer turned away from the screen to face Blake. "So what exactly is this plan of yours?"

"Simple, really," he said. "See, when I was in contact with the undersea colony, I was able to figure out how their scanners work, and assuming the ones on the mother ship operate on the same basic principles, I should be able to fool them long enough to get us in close."

Danny raised an eyebrow. "Quite a leap, isn't it? Don't you think their technology may have changed a little in six hundred years."

"A lot, actually. But data we picked up when the mother ship swooped in on us suggests the scanners are remarkably similar. It's not like going from a horse drawn carriage to an automobile, it's more like going from a carriage *wheel* to an automobile wheel; same basic design, just a lot of refinement. In this case, the basic scanner design looks the same. Hopefully, the beauty's not just skin deep."

He paused to calibrate the shield frequency of the Stargazer. "That should do it." He smiled, with a nod of satisfaction. "Once we activate our shields, the Silesians shouldn't be able to detect us…at least not right away."

"Not right away?" TC asked.

"Yes," Blake said. "They won't be able to see us as we approach, but once we get close, their sensors will detect the motion, and once that happens we'll probably only have a minute or so before they realize what's causing that motion."

"Great plan," Danny said. "So *if* their technology hasn't changed too much in six hundred years, and *if* we can get close enough without them spotting us, then what? They're a hundred times our mass and loaded with weapons we can't even imagine… and my imagination is pretty damned good."

"But *we* have time travel," Blake said. "We spook them with the unknown. The Silesians are not risk-takers by nature. If there is any chance of failure, they'll retreat."

"And just how do you suppose we *spook* them?"

"No time to explain," Blake said. "We've got to get to the site of the Silesian sphere and engage them within the next four hours. In order to maintain the integrity of the timeline as much as possible, Jennifer made sure we arrived here at the precise moment we originally left Omnicenter. Now, if memory serves me right…"

"If?" Danny smirked.

Blake shot a quick glare in his direction, then continued. "Burnstone said the aliens had given us an ultimatum, and if we weren't able to undo the destruction of their colony by the deadline, they would attack. Bottom line, we have four hours to get to that sphere and convince them to abort their attack, or we're going to see just exactly what their *big humongous butt-kicking* weapons, as Danny so eloquently put it, can do."

He turned to Danny. "Did I get that right?"

"I believe that was the phrasing," Danny said with a smile.

Blake gave a quick nod, then continued. "Now, the shield cloaking system I programmed will only be effective in the dark. If we approach in daylight, it won't be hard for them to spot us…even without scanners. And since the sun will be coming up in approximately two and a half hours at their location, we've got just two hours to get there and another half hour to make our approach before the sunlight gives us away.

"TC," he said, "you take the helm. I'll give you instructions on the way."

"Now hold on just a minute," Danny said, reluctant to give up his pilot's seat. "Nobody gives orders on the *Stargazer* without…"

"Danny," Blake said, taking Stryker firmly by the arm and staring into his eyes with a determination Danny had never seen from him before, "trust me."

There were few people in the universe that Danny would trust blindly. At that moment, he realized that Blake Richards had become one of them.

Danny relinquished his chair to TC.

"Lay in course at maximum speed."

"Course plotted…engaged," TC said as he activated the maneuvering thrusters. The only way to make the trip fast enough without attracting attention would be to ascend above the atmosphere, employ a controlled thruster acceleration, then drop back down in the vicinity of the sphere. TC was an experienced navigator; he knew what to do. "I'll have us within five miles of that sphere in about two hours. We'll make our final approach from there."

"Perfect," Blake said. "Engage shields."

Danny activated the ship's protective energy field. "Engaged."

Within minutes, they were in the dark.

*

As they approached the alien ship, scanners showed the enhanced image of the sphere rapidly increasing in size on the forward viewer.

"It doesn't look like they've detected us," Danny said from the navigation station where he now sat.

"Good," Blake said. "Now, Danny, I need you to retract the viewscreen and lower the plating over the forward window."

The Stargazer, like most Federation ships, was equipped with a clear window behind the forward viewscreen, providing the option of direct observation in case of screen failure. Though far less versatile than a computerized viewscreen, it was a precautionary fail-safe, a back-up system that was rarely, if ever, needed.

Danny hesitated briefly, and then gave the command; as the screen slid away, a direct view of the skies opened up ahead of them. The subtle glow of distant stars above a fading crescent moon was all that disturbed the void.

"So your plan is to ram us into that giant sphere in the dark of night?" TC asked, straining to locate the sphere in the blackness. "Cause if it's not, I could use a little help here."

"Scanners say we're still over a mile away," Danny said.

"Slow us to two percent thrusters," Blake said.

"Done," TC said.

Danny nodded. "Ah, so we're going to ram it *really, really slowly*." He bit back his lower lip. "Good plan."

Blake continued. "Now listen, TC, I need you to concentrate. Your bionic eye – you need to focus on the input you're getting from it."

"Focus how? I just look and I see."

"Close your other eye."

TC complied. "Great. So now I'm flying with one eye closed. Much better."

"Concentrate," Blake repeated. "Concentrate on the violet spectrum. Your bionic eye is capable of processing ultraviolet light, your brain just hasn't learned to recognize it yet. You've got to train your mind to interpret the signal in a meaningful way. It will happen automatically if you just concentrate on the violet hues that you *can* see."

TC stared ahead intently, and a violet glow slowly emerged in the distance. "Yeah," he muttered, "Yeah, I'm starting to see it." The light gradually coalesced into a recognizable form. "Looks like a giant purple golf ball."

"That's how their shields look in the dark," Blake said. "And that's how we're going to get close to them. You're going to pilot us right into one of those dimples, where the energy field is low."

"Look guys," Danny piped in, "I don't know what you two are looking at, but the scanners show a solid energy shield around that thing. If you take us in too close, we're going to go dark. We'll be sitting ducks out there. Even if they somehow don't see us bouncing off their shields, we're not going last too long without life support."

"I know what the sensors show, Danny," Blake said, "but they're wrong. There is a significant drop in energy at multiple points around that vessel, points where a ship like ours can safely get within fifty meters.

"See, their shield system works by deploying multiple generators, spaced evenly around the ship. Each one sends out an energy field that dissipates as it grows further from the source. Picture it like little umbrellas opening up all around the hull. When their shields are at maximum, these umbrellas all overlap and form a solid barrier, but as we all know, nobody keeps their shields at maximum all the time; they'd burn out their reactors. And when the power's turned down a notch, there's a weakness – a dimple of low energy between every three umbrellas where they meet at the edges.

"Now, that ship has been hanging over the Atlantic for quite a while, and they're more than capable of monitoring Earth's weapons. They'll keep their shields low until they perceive a threat."

"Not according to our scans," Danny said, pointing to the monitor. "That thing's rock solid."

"Just a deception," Blake shook his head. "Their system's designed to make those shields look the same to our scanners whether they're fully powered or not."

"Clever buggers," Danny muttered.

"Yup," Blake said, "but as long as they don't see us coming, we'll catch them with their pants down. If we can pick out those dimples, we can get right next to them without getting fried."

"So let's readjust the sensors," Danny offered.

"Not so easy," Blake said with a shake of his head. "And we're short on time, but TC and I can do it with our bionic eyes. We can see the shield's ultraviolet silhouette."

Margo's mouth dropped open. "You have bionic eyes?"

"Childhood accident," Blake quickly covered.

Margo didn't buy it. "But I thought Dr. Lee just invented those things? Didn't you say TC was the first human subject for the android eye?"

"Yes, uh…," Blake cleared his throat, "well…"

"Blake's surgery was a little different," Jennifer interjected. It wasn't really a bionic eye, just an occipital lobe implant that was done to repair a defect in his brain's visual cortex."

"Oh," Margo muttered, trying to figure out what Jennifer had just said. "But I thought…"

"Some other time, Margo," Blake stopped her as he glanced in Jennifer's direction.

"Since TC can see those dimples, he can pilot us in with much more alacrity than you could by relying on sensors, Danny."

Danny grunted, reluctantly acquiescing. "And then what? You gonna torpedo that thing and hope we get away before it explodes?"

"Who said we're going to get away?" Blake said, stone-faced.

The room fell silent, and a uniform look of horror crept across their faces as the meaning of his simple statement sunk in.

"You mean…we're going to blow ourselves up!" Margo yelped.

"If it's the only way we can take these bastards out, "Danny said, "then let's get on with it."

"Gotcha!" Blake burst out laughing. "If you all could have seen the looks on your faces…"

No one else was amused.

"All right, all right." Blake waved a hand. "Look, I have no intention of committing suicide."

"Then what?" TC asked.

"Just get us to our target while I get ready. It'll be easier to show you." Blake turned and walked into the short corridor that led back to the sleeping quarters.

Danny and Jennifer looked at each other, and then hurried after Blake, catching up as he was about to enter Danny's room, where his pack was stowed.

Danny grabbed Blake by the shoulder. "If you ever pull something like that again…" he said, gritting his teeth. His squinted face slowly morphed into a broad grin. "I'll take you to the nearest bar and buy you a drink." He slapped him on the shoulder. "Didn't think you had it in you, man."

Blake smiled.

"Neither did I," Jennifer muttered with a hint of disgust.

"Sorry, Jen. I just couldn't resist. Look, you two go back out there and make sure Margo's behaving. I don't want her distracting TC. I'll be out in a second."

They complied, and Blake ducked into Danny's quarters to get his pack.

*

Steven Kolanski anxiously paced the floor of the Communications Center at Space Corps Command. It had been over two hours since the

Stargazer had departed from Omnicenter to make the jump back to the twentieth century.

General Burnstone stood by the scanner's giant glass monitor, looking over Lieutenant Myers' shoulder.

"Kolanski!" he barked, turning to face Ski. "Would you stop that incessant pacing? You're driving the lieutenant here nuts."

Myers glanced back over his shoulder at the general. "Actually, it's not the pacing that's making me nervous, sir."

"Huh," Burnstone muttered. He turned back to face the screen, and was practically nose to nose with the lieutenant. "Oh…uh…right." He leaned away, but kept his eyes trained on the scans. "Where the hell are they? If everything went OK, they should have been back almost before they left. They are in a time machine, for God's sake."

Kolanski walked over and stood on the other side of the lieutenant. "We gave them the same four hour cushion the fish people gave us. I'm sure Stryker's got his reasons for using those hours."

"He sure as hell better. Knowing those two clowns, they're probably doing this just to make us sweat."

Lieutenant Myers snickered. Stryker and McGee's antics were legendary.

"Something amusing, son," Burnstone sneered.

"Uh, no, sir." Myers bit back his amusement. "Still nothing on the scans, sir."

"I can see that," Burnstone said sharply. "I may be old, but I'm not…"

"Wait," Myers interrupted.

The three men stared at the screen. Something was approaching the sphere from the west. The blip was unrecognizable to Kolanski and Burnstone, but there was a reason Myers was manning the Comm Center.

"That's them, sir."

"What do you mean that's them? That's not a Federation signature."

"Yes, sir. It is," Myers said. "I mean, it's not, but…" He paused and tapped a few buttons on the panel in front of him. "If you factor out a theoretical dampening field oscillating at an ascending frequency of… There!" he yelled with a gleam in his eye.

The blip on the screen changed to a light shade of blue, the computer equivalent of a Federation energy signature.

"Well, I'll be," Burnstone muttered. "Damn fine work, son."

"Thank you, sir." Lieutenant Myers did not turn around, but Ski could see him beaming. The lieutenant had redeemed himself from his prior error in record time. Kolanski nodded his approval in silence.

*

Blake walked onto the bridge, fumbling with a thick bracelet on his left wrist. "What's our position?"

TC glanced at his screen. "Three hundred meters and closing."

Jennifer was the first to notice. "Quigley's holoprojector? It was a pretty good trick getting that thing to work two miles under the ocean, but at least there you were right next to the sphere. There's no way that's going to project across space. Even if TC can maneuver us in as close as you say, we'll still be fifty meters out, and right next to some pretty powerful field generators."

"Not necessarily," TC said, admiring the view provided by his new eye. The purple hue of the energy field was sharply in focus now. It was beautiful. "I can ease us within a few meters of one of those dimples, no sweat. The energy arc is so precise that we can steer clear of any fluctuations, and those generators are right on the surface. Hell, I can get us within ten meters of the hull."

Blake smiled. "Let's not get carried away. Fifty meters is all I need. This baby," he tapped his wrist, "will work just fine from there."

"Yeah," TC's eyes widened, "but I can do it…really; it'll be fun. Hang on to something."

Blake placed a hand firmly on TC's shoulder. "Not a good idea. Once I make contact, I intend to rattle them and we're going to need a little cushion to get out of here in one piece."

"Wait, wait, wait." Danny waved a hand. "Come again? You want to spook those bastards? Look at them!" He pointed out the window. The sphere was easily a hundred times the size of the Stargazer. "Are you nuts?"

Blake turned to Danny. "It's the only way…or at least our best shot. One way or another, we've got to get them to leave Earth, and I don't think our weapons are going to scare them off. The way I see it, we have only one trump card, and I intend to use it."

"Time travel," Jennifer said.

Blake nodded. "Look, they aren't going to like what I have to say, and they certainly aren't going to be real thrilled that we managed to sneak up on them. I don't know exactly how they're going to react, but I suspect they're not going to want to hang around too long to chat."

Blake looked over TC's shoulder at the scanner; they were closing on fifty meters. "OK. Ease her into position."

TC's fingers continued to dance rapidly across the helm control panel, his full attention focused on negotiating the purple maze.

"TC?"

He hesitated briefly, then his hands gradually slowed to a stop and he let out a deep breath. "We're in position."

Blake stepped up to the window. "Now get ready to close the front shields and punch out of here on my mark."

"On it," Danny said.

Blake looked back at his friends. "And you may want to cover your ears."

Chapter Sixteen:
First contact…Again

Blake donned a small headset with a single vid-flap, which he swung down over his right eye. Turning back toward the sphere, he activated the holoprojector.

The headset was his own addition to Quigley's little marvel. Blake's first use of the holoprojector at the undersea colony had been both fascinating and extraordinarily frustrating at the same time. Although he'd been able to throw his image into the Silesian colony, he was totally blind once inside. It was a frustration he vowed not to repeat.

Although this journey had given Blake precious little time to tinker with Quigley's toy, he had managed to steal an hour or so of solitude while they were making their way over from Pearl Harbor, and used it to jury-rig a photon video camera into the holoprojector.

This elegantly simple device was something he'd developed to combat isolation during his exile on the moon of Kennedy Prime, and was capable of bringing back images from anything that could be reached with a photon beam by simply bouncing light particles off an object, and then returning those particles through the same beam. It was easily adaptable to Quigley's device, and piggy-backing a sound generator would give him full virtual reality capability.

Blake carefully positioned his likeness inside the Silesian mother ship, easing through the delicate aquatic environment. The sensation of floating as if suspended in glycerin, something that could have been relaxing under different circumstances, left him feeling uncomfortably out of control. He found himself in a storage center near the ship's periphery, lined with cabinets that shimmered through the liquid. An opalescent glow emanated from a small opening in the otherwise barren wall to his right, and he wandered over, reaching out for it.

Euphoria overwhelmed him, raw data flowing faster than his brain could assimilate. He drank it in, storing it for later analysis.

The value of the data was incalculable, but it was critical that he make contact with one of the Silesians before the Stargazer's position was discovered.

Forcing himself away from the data console, he glided through a circular portal leading to a voluminous chamber unbounded by floors or walls, with the exception of variously shaped irregular planes of a blue metallic substance jutting about at right angles where needed to support various pieces of unrecognizable equipment.

Blake emerged into a room teeming with activity. There were easily over a hundred Silesians suspended effortlessly around various consoles projecting from the fragments of walls, floors and ceilings, though none of the structures formed a complete room. Dozens more were gathered around a cylindrical object in the center of the chamber. Everything shimmered icy-blue in the viscous atmosphere. Blake hung motionless just outside the portal, mesmerized by the surreal vision.

His solitude did not last long.

A harsh trill emanated from the first of the Silesians to spot him, followed by a cacophony of squeals and shrieks that nearly knocked him from his precariously balanced position. He spun back and reached for his ears.

The sudden motion of his gesture stilled the room.

He straightened and turned to face them. Some of the larger ones began to move tentatively in his direction; security guards, Blake surmised. He raised his arms and all motion ceased. The room fell absolutely silent.

Dozens of pairs of large black eyes focused squarely upon him. Blake stared them down with the confidence of a man who knew his body was not in the line of fire. The aliens held their ground, studying him intently like a pack of dogs sizing up a new adversary.

The stand-off was brief.

One of them resumed its cautious approach, its pale yellow body flagellating slowly in the surrounding blue liquid with just a hint of trepidation in its erratic movement. One by one, the followers began to join in. Blake realized his time was limited.

"We *have* been to the past and back," he said emphatically. The aliens halted in mid stroke, unlike any motion their human counterparts could mimic. "We *know* what you did to the colonists and we find your actions reprehensible. You have called us barbaric because of the criminal act of one person, yet you plotted the murder of hundreds of your own kind."

He paused, waiting for a response.

It came by way of a deeply pitched voice breaking through from behind a small grouping of the entities gathered closest to him. "On what do you base your accusations?" The group parted as a somewhat smaller and more weathered appearing creature floated through to approach him. "I see no proof that you have traveled into the past."

Blake gritted his teeth. "You are the commander of this vessel?"

The alien tilted the top half of its torso in Blake's direction; *a nod*. It moved in closer.

Blake fought the urge to back away from the advancing menace of authority, and stood fast as it flipped a fin in his direction. Blake could see the image of his own body waver in the microcurrents created by the action.

The alien didn't seem surprised. "Very impressive for such a primitive species, but time travel?" It warbled and looked back toward the group, who mimicked the sound.

Laughter? "Then how do you think we were able to fool your sensors?"

As soon as the words left his mouth, he regretted them. The Silesians obviously hadn't considered that Blake was broadcasting his likeness from close range. The ruse had worked, but the deception wasn't likely to hold up against closer scrutiny. The alien turned quickly and motioned to one of the others, who darted over to a console in the center of the atrium and began to run one of its webbed hands over the device.

It was just a matter of time until the Stargazer's position was compromised. He could only hope that the ship's proximity to the field generator would continue to fool the scanners until he finished delivering his message.

"Surely," Blake resumed, "you don't think we have the technology to penetrate your shields so readily. You have scanned our cities; you know our capabilities."

"And we see no evidence of your ability to master time."

"There is a lot you don't see," Blake responded. "We conceal our strategic information as well as you do."

The Silesian captain suspended himself in front of Blake without saying a word, motionless except for a barely perceptible vibration of a fin now and then.

Blake's penetrating glare did not waver. "Think about it. Without the information we got from your colonists, how could we have learned to fool your sensors and project this transmission into your ship? How could we know that the probe you prepared to save your colonists was rigged to blow up as soon as they took off?"

The captain stared in silence as the group of security goons behind him began to close in. Blake could feel himself leaning away; even knowing his body wasn't actually in harm's way, it was still difficult to convince his innate mechanism of self-preservation that the threat was not real.

Finally, the captain shifted position; *another nod*? "A good point. In fact, if you had attempted to scan the probe, it would have triggered a self-destruct and we would not be having this conversation."

Blake shook his head. "It would have been nice to mention that when you gave it to us."

The alien wriggled and warbled again. "But not as amusing."

Blake was dumbfounded. *A joke*?

The captain's body shifted upright. The game of cat and mouse was about to resume. "You must share with us the secrets of time propulsion," he said. "We have much of value to offer in exchange."

"And you must realize that your request cannot be granted. Against technology as advanced as yours, controlling time is our most effective defense."

"But we are a peaceful race," the captain pleaded.

"I witnessed the beneficence of your 'peaceful ways' over five hundred years in our past. I do not wish to witness more. You may leave our world, but go with the knowledge that we control time. If you decide to become less *beneficent* towards us, we have only to contact our operatives in prior time periods to undo whatever damage you may inflict."

Blake was confident the Silesians had no idea how restrictive the Federation was when it came to the use of time travel, but a little embellishment could be a healthy thing when employed at the right time.

"You will not hear from us again," the captain said. "If you have learned anything of our nature from your scans, you must know that we shun contact with terrestrials. This confrontation was a matter of self-preservation, nothing more."

Blake knew that the captain spoke the truth, but the promise of time travel technology was a powerful lure. He hoped the Silesians' xenophobia would outweigh their thirst to obtain it.

"Then go in peace," Blake said.

He watched briefly as the Silesian captain turned and darted away, presumably toward the bridge, though it was hard to say given the seemingly random jumble of equipment scattered around the sphere's interior. All the other aliens followed, and Blake realized that as much as he would like to stay and study their technology, it would be more prudent to withdrawal immediately.

*

Blake flipped the eyepiece up, and his consciousness was once again on the bridge of the Stargazer. He staggered slightly, then shook off the disorientation and turned to TC.

"Get us out of here – *now*!" He ran to his chair at the comm station. "Everybody to stations."

Jennifer and Margo hurried back to Danny's quarters to secure themselves in.

Danny watched as the sphere began to oscillate, growing larger with each pulse.

"Stargazer!" he barked out. "Close forward shields and reactivate viewscreen."

"Affirmative," came the incongruously calm reply.

As the shields snapped shut, TC had already spun the ship 180 degrees, but they seemed to be moving away at a snail's pace.

"TC!" Danny snapped.

TC's gaze darted back and forth between the aft viewer and his scanners. "Still too close," he yelled.

The sphere began to turn a reddish violet color, pulsating so rapidly that the motion was almost imperceptible.

"Come on, come on," TC muttered through clenched teeth. "Eighteen Hundred…Nineteen Hundred… *Now! Full thrusters!*"

Pinned to the back of his seat, Danny peered into the aft viewer, searching. "Where the hell did it go?"

A vague distortion slowly rippled into view in the center of the screen. Blake was the first to recognize the telltale signs of an impulse wake; a surge of energy ten times larger than the sphere had been generated by its rapid acceleration and was now heading directly towards Earth with the *Stargazer* dead center in its path.

"Oh crap."

Chapter Seventeen:
It's all Relative

"Come on!" Danny yelled. "Punch it."

"Already topped out." TC was fighting to maneuver the ship away from the shock wave at a ninety degree angle.

"Switch to impulse."

"Too close to Earth."

The shock wave was closing fast.

"*TC?!*"

"Brace for impact."

Secured into their seats, or, in Margo's case, the bunk in Danny's quarters, they dug their nails into whatever they could as the *Stargazer* was pounded by the kinetic pulse.

The ship lurched sharply to the right, and then shuddered as its stabilizers fought to maintain position. Maneuvering capabilities were hampered by Earth's atmosphere and they were catapulted away at a thirty-degree angle, flipping end over end as Danny and TC struggled to regain control.

"Stabilizers are off line," the computer announced.

"No kidding!" Danny sniped. "Give me manual."

"Manual control engaged."

Danny strained against the g-forces of the spin, trying to maintain focus and regain control of the ship. He tapped the panel several times, but there was no response. "Manual's off-line too," he yelled to TC. "You're going to have to use thruster bursts to counteract the spin."

"I don't know if she can take it this close in; we've still got atmosphere out there."

"Got a better idea?"

"Yeah." TC strained to right himself in his chair. "We should be clear in about fifteen seconds."

"How the hell can you tell? I don't even know which way is up."

"Still got sensors," TC said, straining to focus on the readout in front of him. "We're almost there."

Once clear of the atmosphere, TC was able to regain control and the ship began to settle into a normal attitude. A sense of relief spread throughout the crew.

"Everybody OK back there?" Danny called through the comm.

"Sure," Margo mumbled, "just as soon as we clean the *puke* off your bed."

His face blanched.

Snickers wafted through the comm.

"Very amusing." He shut off the channel.

TC pried his hands off the armrests, rubbing the circulation back into his pale fingertips. He looked down at his display. "Uh-oh."

Danny glanced askew. "Now what?"

"Thrusters are down."

"What about impulse?"

"Nope. Tried that too. We're drifting free."

The computer interrupted. "Stabilizers are back on-line."

"Great," Danny said. "At least we can drift in a straight line."

TC shook his head. "Maybe not."

"Come again?"

Blake was one step ahead of Danny. "We didn't quite reach orbital altitude, did we?"

TC shook his head.

"How long until our orbit decays?"

"Already happening. Shields are holding, so we can take the heat, but I'd say we've got about twenty minutes before we hit the ground. The good news is that Earth seems unscathed; the atmosphere deflected the whole thing."

A facetious smile creased Danny's face. "Well, that certainly makes *me* feel better. Think we can avoid making a dent when we hit. Be a shame to mar the surface after all that."

"Maybe we'll land in the ocean," TC offered.

"Great. So if we survive the impact, we'll drown."

"She might hold out water long enough for us to take the shuttle topside."

Jennifer interrupted. "Uh…guys?"

Danny glanced at the speaker on his panel where Jennifer's voice had come from. "Right. Stargazer," he called out, "damage report."

"Engines are off-line. Detecting cracks in the casings of both thruster and impulse engines. Emergency shut-down initiated."

"Well, uninitiate. It'll take us an hour to get them back on line."

"Risk of explosion is greater than ninety percent."

"Can the cracks be repaired?"

"Yes."

"Great," Danny said with a sigh of relief. "How long will it take?"

"With available equipment, approximately fourteen hours."

"Oh yeah," TC said. "That's a big help."

"Well," Danny said, "I'm open to suggestions."

"Fifteen minutes until impact," the ship announced.

"Right," Danny said. "Any *useful* suggestions."

"Stargazer?" Blake asked. "Do we still have enough power to activate time-warp?"

"Affirmative."

"Great idea," TC said. "So we can just jump out of this time-line and smack into Earth sometime in the past."

"Or the future," Danny added, nodding. "Lots of choices."

"Or perhaps to a time when Earth is not next to us in space," Blake said.

"It's a time-jump," Danny said. "We stay in the same place in space. I thought you were supposed to be smart."

"Wait," Jennifer's voice came through the comm. "Blake's right. When I calculate a time-jump, I have to adjust for the movement of the planets. That's why it takes so long to set up. But if we ignore the planetary movement, we can jump into the same space we're in now, regardless of where the planet is."

"And six months ago," Blake added, "Earth was on the other side of the sun, half way through a solar cycle."

"Cool," TC said. "So we just jump back six months and we'll be free and clear."

"With plenty of time to fix those engines," Jennifer added.

"Nine minutes until impact," the ship announced.

"Jen, how long will it take you to…"

"Be ready to jump in five minutes."

"Cutting it a bit close, aren't we?"

"Wouldn't be any fun if I didn't."

The oppressive grip of the increasing g-forces squeezed like a vice as they spiraled toward the planet, but no one said a word for fear of distracting Jennifer.

Finally, her voice ripped through the deafening silence. "Brace for time-jump…*Now!*"

Time went blank.

*

TC gathered himself and checked the fore and aft viewers – nothing but stars. He breathed a sigh of relief, and could sense the ship beginning to slow.

Danny hopped out of his chair. "Let's get on those repairs."

*

It would take all of the fourteen hours the computer predicted to effect repairs. Danny set the ship on autopilot and headed to the engine room to join

TC; he could monitor their position from there. While he and TC worked on repairs, Blake began deciphering the data he had downloaded from archives aboard the sphere, leaving Margo feeling useless; she sneaked off to TC's quarters to grab some rest.

Jennifer activated the holographic keyboard at the workstation in Danny's room; she found the quaint interface less distracting than trying to talk her way through the math. Calculations for the next jump would be tricky; in order to minimize risk of time distortion, she wanted to make sure they arrived back as close as possible to the exact time and place they had left, while staying clear of the kinetic burst generated by the Silesian sphere.

Within a few hours, Blake had translated all of the data and went to find Jennifer. He smiled as he peered through the open door of Danny's quarters and saw her typing away.

She stopped and looked back over her shoulder.

"Heard me coming, huh?"

"Nah," she shook her head, "felt you."

He motioned to the keyboard. "I thought that was a lost art."

"What can I say? I'm an artist."

"That you are."

She leaned back and thrust her delicate arms into the air with an audible sigh, sending a wave of silky black hair cascading behind as she stretched. "So," she whispered through a yawn, "what's up?"

His smile faded. "You aren't going to believe what I found."

*

Once full systems were up and running, it proved relatively easy to make the jump and guide the *Stargazer* back to Africa unscathed. The final approach into Omnicenter wouldn't take long.

TC, back at the helm, looked hesitantly in Danny's direction. "Want your chair back?"

"Nah," Danny said, wrapping his hands behind his head and settling back comfortably. "Go ahead. I think I could get used to this."

"In a pig's eye," TC muttered as he reached for the piloting interface.

Danny chuckled and looked over at Blake, who was sitting back at the comm. station. "Hail Space Corps Command. Tell them we're on our way. I'm sure Ski is sweating bullets by now. I can't wait to hear how you're going to explain this all to him."

"Me! Oh, no," Blake shook his head. "I'm just a lowly civilian. Besides, I've got to keep my distance from those guys, remember?" He hadn't noticed Margo coming up behind him.

"Yeah," she eyed him suspiciously, "about that…"

Blake spun awkwardly fumbling for the right words. "I…uh…"

"Oh come on, Blake. I may act like an airhead sometimes, but give me some credit, would you? I'm getting a little tired of pretending like I don't know what's going on around here."

Blake was dumbfounded. "You knew?

She nodded.

"How long?"

"Seems like forever."

He stood silently for a moment, staring at the floor, then sighed and looked up. "Then I've got to go. I can't be around you anymore; it's just too dangerous."

"Of course it is, you big nerd; that's why you need me. This whole charade of yours will be a lot more believable if *I'm* along for the ride."

He shook his head. "I won't put your life in danger."

"I can live with the danger," she said without hesitation.

He looked into her eyes. "Do you know what they'll do if they discover you're harboring an *android* in Federation territory?"

"Android!" Margo stumbled back. "You're an *android*?"

Blake's jaw dropped open. "But," he sputtered, "if you didn't know, then…"

Margo burst out laughing. "Of course I knew. You are *so* pathetic when it comes to keeping secrets. That's exactly why you need me, and you're not going anywhere without me. Not anymore."

Blake avoided her smile. "At least if I'm gone, you can deny you ever knew about it. Everyone here will back you up."

"Oh, *who* are *you* kidding?" Margo leaned forward and lifted his chin inches from her own. "You want me, Blake Richards. And everyone in this room knows it. You want me and I want you. It's as simple as that."

He cleared his throat and stood. "For God's sake, Margo. I'm your teacher."

"Oh, give…me…a…break," she said. "Look, I'm your research assistant, not some bleary-eyed teenager. I'm twenty-seven years old. How old are you? All of thirty? Heck, you look more like you're about twenty-two. People are going to think *I'm* the one robbing the cradle in this relationship."

"Relationship?"

"Yeah, relationship," she said, slipping her arms around him.

Blake looked into her dark brown eyes, and all protest evaporated from his soul as he relaxed into her embrace. The warmth of her lips revived sensations he'd long ago abandoned hope of ever feeling again.

Margo sighed serenely. "You don't know how long I've been waiting to do that."

Blake pulled away feebly. "Look, Margo. This can't work. I'll never grow old."

"So? What, you'll be embarrassed to be seen with me when *I'm* old?" She scowled through a thinly veiled smile. "I'll still be way cooler than you, even when I'm old and wrinkled."

"No doubt." He smiled sheepishly. "But people will realize. Our friends will see that I'm not aging, and they'll get curious. I can't ever stay in one place for too long and I can't risk having too many friends."

"Well, heck," Danny interrupted, "you can never have *too* many friends."

Jennifer smacked him on the arm.

Blake barely glanced in his direction, and then looked back at Margo. "What kind of life will that be for you?"

"Exactly the one I want…as long as I'm with you." Margo's resolve was firm.

"And besides," Blake looked down and shook his head, "it's just too hard. I don't know if I can do it again."

"Do what?" Margo asked.

"I don't want to outlive my family again."

"I wish I could do something about that, Blake, but I can't. All I can promise is that I'll be here for you as long as I can, and that I'll love you until the day I die. I'm sorry that you'll have to live through that, but it's just part of life, and you *are* alive. The only alternative is to not love, not be a part of anyone else's life, and to do that… that would *not* be living."

Blake pulled her close. "It *is* nice to feel like this again."

Chapter Eighteen:
Aftershock

"Vanished! What do you mean it vanished?" General Burnstone put down his coffee mug and rushed toward the monitor, peering over Lieutenant Meyers' shoulder.

"Just that, sir. I had it on sensors, then it just dropped off the screen."

Burnstone squinted in vain.

"Right there." Myers wagged a finger at a spot toward the upper left side of the grid. "Those bastards were just sitting there all that time; not so much as a wobble out of them. I don't know how the hell they did it. It takes a truckload of energy to do something like that, but my scans weren't picking up squat; nothing out of them for hours. Then all of a sudden there was this massive power surge. I glanced over to check my readings and by the time I looked back they were gone. No ship, no energy signature, nothing. I just *lost* 'em."

Kolanski, having just returned from a pit stop, joined the conversation. "What do you mean you just *lost* them? Didn't you track their trajectory?"

"There wasn't any. It just disappeared from sensors, then a few seconds later I picked up a huge shock wave coming back at us."

"Damages?" Ski asked.

Myers deftly ran his fingers over the panel in front of him. "The atmosphere soaked up most of it, probably not much other than some rough seas in the north Atlantic. I doubt anyone even noticed"

Burnstone smoothed back his hair. "So what happened to the bastards anyway? They just blow up?"

Myers shook his head emphatically. "No way. That shock wave had to be some kind of kick-back from their engines. If they blew up, there would have been one hell of a blast. We couldn't have missed something like that."

"We couldn't have missed a ship the size of Capetown Stadium taking off, either," Kolanski said.

Myers tilted his head in Kolanski's direction. "That's assuming they use a propulsion system like ours, which isn't very likely. That thing can stop on a dime from near light speed and I'd wager a few bucks they can accelerate just as quickly. Whatever they use, we can't track it."

"And what about the Stargazer," grunted Burnstone. "Any sign of it?"

Meyers studied the monitor again, then tapped a few icons on the control module.

"Enhancing scanners to maximize...*there!*" He pointed to a small blip on the screen. "That's them."

"Good." Burnstone stood up, stretching his stiff back, then pulled down on the bottom of his jacket to straighten the lines. "I want them in my office the second they get back."

"Yes, sir," Kolanski said.

He watched the general walk out, and then turned his attention to the monitor and followed the course of Stryker's ship across the screen. "That man's got nine lives," he said. "Hail them and tell them to meet me in A-17."

"Aye, sir."

Kolanski started to walk away, then stopped and turned. "Oh, and good work, son."

A subtle grin crept across the face of the young lieutenant. "Thank you, sir," he said, never taking his eyes off of the scanner as the colonel's footsteps tracked out the door.

The communications room was Lieutenant Myers' private domain once again.

*

"There she is, folks," TC said. Omnicenter was visible on the forward viewscreen.

"Look, Blake," Danny said. "The three of us can handle the debriefing. The less exposure you have to these guys the better. Obviously, that vest Jennifer rigged up for you fooled the scanners last time, but sooner or later something's going to blow your cover."

"I'm pretty sure Quigley's already figured it out," Blake said.

TC let out a grunt. "Probably right. Nothing gets past that weirdo."

"Hey!" Jennifer had a fond place in her heart for Quigley.

"I meant that in a *good* way."

"Yeah, right. Look, I know he's a little different…"

"Ah-hah!"

"In a *good* way," she added.

Danny cleared his throat. "Right, anyhow, with all the distractions last time we were there, I doubt anybody *else* noticed. But this time all of their attention is going to be on us."

"So what do we do about Quigley?" Blake asked.

"Quigley's probably OK with this even if he does suspect," Jennifer said. "He likes knowing something that he's not supposed to, especially if no one else does. But he still may not be completely sure and I don't want to give him a second look at you."

"Hey, you've got no argument here, but won't they be expecting me for the debriefing?"

"Hell," Danny said, "you're less military than I am. You don't have to answer to those guys."

"I don't want to piss them off, either."

"Ah, don't worry about it. Ski will be a little steamed at first, but they're used to it when I don't follow protocol. Let me handle it. You just get Margo back to Woods Hole on the shuttle. I'll make your excuses – I'll tell them they've threatened to fire you if you don't get her back there today."

"Not so far from the truth." Blake shook his head.

"Then you're worrying about the wrong guys," Danny grinned. "Look, Ski and Burnstone, they trust me and TC enough to let us handle the debriefing... well, at least as long as Jennifer is with us." He smiled in her direction and she responded with a knowing gleam in her eye.

"We won't contact you again for a while. You two go on about your normal lives up there until Margo finishes her doctorate. When you're ready, I'm sure we can find you work on Kennedy Prime – both of you, if that's what you want. It's still the Federation, but things are a lot looser out there. It attracts a different breed of people, you know? Pioneers tend to like their privacy."

"Thanks, Danny."

"Don't mention it. Hell, it'd be nice to have you around to pick on more often."

*

TC piloted the *Stargazer* into the steel city.

"Sure is a relief to see this place without a dome over it."

"Yeah," Danny said. "That was *not* my idea of what the future should look like."

Jennifer agreed. "Maybe we should send the Silesians a thank you note."

Danny raised an eyebrow. "That'd be like thanking somebody for shooting you in the leg to scratch an itch."

TC chuckled. "Look, Blake, I'm going to drop you two off at the civilian field as close as I can get to your shuttle, but the brass are going to be pretty miffed when they see me landing their time-warp generator out there, so get your stuff together and be ready to hop off the second I land. As soon as you're clear, I'm getting this thing back to A-17."

"Right," Blake said.

Margo needed no prodding. She quickly gathered her things.

"Thanks for putting up with me, guys," she shouted from the doorway to the bridge.

TC grunted and turned his head just enough for Margo to see that he had done it with a smile.

"Same to you," she winked.

"Just take care of our boy there," TC said.

Margo looked over her shoulder at Blake, who had just walked up behind her. "Won't take my eyes off him," she called back.

Danny tipped his head in her direction, then turned his attention back to the scanners.

Jennifer walked over and gave her a hug. "Take care," she said. "If you do decide to come to K-Prime, look me up. We could use someone like you at the Center."

"If all goes well. Thanks."

*

The *Stargazer* eased down onto the landing field about sixty meters from the Woods Hole shuttle. With her engines still purring, the landing ramp telescoped to the ground and Blake quickly made his way out with Margo. They didn't stop running until they reached the shuttle; with the entry stairs descending toward them, Blake glanced back over his shoulder shielding his eyes from the sun as the larger ship floated back into the air and headed toward Bay A-17 where an impatient Steven Kolanski would be waiting.

Chapter Nineteen:
Of Past and Future Demons

The Stargazer's landing system created a nearly silent suction effect above the ship, suspending the massive vessel motionless over the landing bay and then gracefully easing her to the ground. As she entered A-17, the faint odor of spent engine fuel seeped into the surrounding air. Although the noisy thrusters were disengaged during the final approach, the smell of a recently fired thruster was unmistakable and it always brought back fond memories of space flight to Kolanski.

The door slipped open and a ramp dropped to the ground from the ship's midsection. Jennifer exited first, followed by TC and Danny.

"Cutting it a bit close, aren't we?" Kolanski said. They had used every bit of the four hour window allotted for the mission.

"As always," Danny said with his characteristic smile.

"You'd think someone who can manipulate time could manipulate himself back here a little earlier."

"Yeah," Danny winked. "You'd think so, wouldn't you?"

"Can't wait to hear your explanation." Kolanski looked past his three friends, back toward the hatch. "Aren't we missing a couple of people?"

"Yeah," TC said, "about that…"

"We dropped them off in the parking lot," Danny said.

"Aw, c'mon guys. You know the drill. Everyone on the mission reports for debriefing unless otherwise stipulated by the CO."

"Blake's not Space Corps," Jennifer said. "Neither is the Feldman girl. Blake was under the gun to get her back to Wood's Hole pronto or risk losing his job. It was my call, and I said let him go."

"Great!" Kolanski said. "The general's going to have my ass over this."

"Ah, don't worry," Danny said, "I doubt he really wants it."

Kolanski flipped him a sardonic smile. "Let's go," he said, turning toward the door.

They followed closely behind as Kolanski led them to the office where Burnstone was waiting impatiently. Quigley was already there, sitting at a coffee table perusing a technical journal.

"About time," the general snapped, glancing up from his desk and peering past the four Space Corps officers. He was about to open his mouth when Kolanski beat him to the punch.

"I sent the two civvies back to Woods Hole. They've got nothing to add that we can't get out of these three, and the less of our conversation they hear the better."

The general hesitated briefly, then responded with a terse nod of the head. "Let's get started."

Kolanski turned and motioned the others toward a grouping of chairs around a coffee table. They made their way over and waited for the general to join them.

Burnstone stood from his desk, gave a quick tug to straighten his uniform jacket and walked over. As he sat, he motioned for the others to do the same, then folded his arms across his chest. "All right. Who wants to go first?"

Danny started the debriefing, with Jennifer and TC interrupting at times to correct some of the minor flaws in his version of what had taken place. Within fifteen minutes, they had covered the events of the mission in adequate detail.

"And you did all that in four hours." Burnstone nodded his approval.

"You're still thinking three dimensionally, General," Jennifer said. "What was four hours for you was over nineteen for us. We were..."

"I'm not *totally* daft, young lady," the general sputtered. "I was speaking metaphorically. I'm well aware of the incongruities *and* the implications of time travel, and frankly, it scares the hell out of me. I want that time-warp generator disassembled."

Kolanski turned and studied Burnstone's face. Military men were usually the last to even consider putting the lid on anything that could yield a tactical advantage, no matter what the consequences.

"Begging your pardon, General," Jennifer said, "but I don't think that's such a good idea."

Now it was Jennifer's turn to draw the shocked looks. She had been one of the most outspoken people against expanding the time warp program in spite of her role in developing the technology. She had always urged that access be strictly limited.

Danny leaned forward. "Excuse me?"

"Shortly before we landed, I met with Blake. He had just finished interpreting the data he recorded from the Silesian ship."

Quigley's head popped up from the journal that had been drawing more of his attention than the mundane details of the mission up till now. "I thought you said he had holoprojected his image into their vessel."

"I did."

"Then explain to me how his holoprojected image managed to retrieve data and send it back to the Stargazer."

"Well, uh...," Jennifer stumbled for the words. She could hardly explain that Blake had managed to augment Quigley's device in a matter of hours. A marine biologist would never have the skills to do something like that. Jennifer barely understood the modifications herself. "I...uh, adapted your holoprojector with a photonic feedback loop so it could gather data and send it back to a recorder I linked into the visor."

Quigley raised an eyebrow. He had been working on just such a modification himself for the past three months without success, and though Jennifer was a brilliant scientist, her skills paled in comparison to his. "Very impressive."

She squirmed under the scrutiny of his unwavering eyes, and a wry grin began to creep across his lips. "You'll have to go over the specs with me later."

Burnstone was fidgeting with the silver-plated pen that usually decorated his chest pocket, a gift from his wife when he'd made general. He had scrounged up something to write on to give it a try that first day, but never found a need for it since then other than to occupy his hands at times like these. "So what did he find?"

Jennifer was clearly relieved by Burnstone's redirection, but then concern creased her forehead. "Some pretty disturbing stuff."

Danny leaned forward. "And just when were you and Blake going to let *us* in on this?"

"You guys were busy fixing the engines," she said. "I figured you would have just been annoyed by Blake's esoterica again."

"Can't argue with that."

Jennifer continued, "It seems the Silesians have known about us for quite some time."

Kolanski raised an eyebrow. "No kidding. We've already been through the *Titanic* thing."

Jennifer waved him off. "That was just the tip of the…" She caught herself and cleared her throat, fighting off a smile. "Look, when Blake got access to their archives, it fed him the most recently accessed data first – all their historical records of contact with Earth. Their first trip here was about sixty-five million years ago."

"Sixty-five *million*!" Kolanski gaped. "Come on. Anybody who's been around that long wouldn't be wasting time playing games with us. We'd be insects to them."

"Well, it wasn't *them*, exactly. See, several hundred years ago, they discovered evidence that a prior species called the Iktai had inhabited their planet, and some of those archives were still intact."

"For millions of years?" Danny shook his head. "No data lasts that long."

"Nothing we've come up with. But that hardly means it's impossible."

"Even so, if you found something like that, you wouldn't understand it. You'd have no frame of reference for the language, much less for the type of technology they used."

"True, but as technology advances, the ultimate goal is to make it user-friendly enough so that you don't *need* to be able to understand it to make it work. Maybe what the Silesians found was so sophisticated that once it heard them talking, it learned their language and talked back."

"Wish it all worked that way."

"Not in my lifetime," Quigley laughed. "If I let that happen, I'll be out of a job."

Burnstone twirled his pen a few more times. "So what did they find?"

"It seems the Iktai came here millions of years ago in their search for new worlds to colonize. Like the Silesians, the Iktai were aquatic, so Earth seemed like a perfect fit. Only when they got here, they found the place crawling with dinosaurs. They decided to clean it up and diverted a huge asteroid to collide with Earth."

"And we know how that worked out," Danny said. "So why didn't they come back?"

"Not sure. The records just stop. Something wiped them out; the whole species. But when the Silesians learned of a planet that was seventy percent water and had had all life purged from it millions of years ago, they came looking for us.

"When they found us, about six hundred years ago, we were already entering the industrial age; exactly the type of world they like to avoid. So they quarantined us; placed Earth off-limits to any future exploration."

TC glanced up. "Why? Seems like we would have been an easy target."

"Well, we know they had bad luck with terrestrials before, but maybe it's more than that. Their historical records *seem* to back up what they say." She dipped her head and paused before continuing on, slowly, deliberately. "Everything I saw, everything Blake dug up from their archives *does* suggest they are a peaceful race. Maybe they just didn't want a mass killing on their hands."

Danny squirmed. "Oh, come on. They tried to kill their own colonists, for God's sake."

"True," Jennifer said. "And after all, history *is* written by the winners. I'm not so sure I trust them either. But for whatever reason, they chose to stay away. Of course, the fact that Earth was placed off-limits by their government was reason enough for many Silesians to pursue it."

"And one of those morons crashed into the *Titanic* in the twentieth century," TC said.

"Right. And here we are."

Burnstone's eyes narrowed. "And just *why* was this all so important?"

"Because we know about them now," Jennifer said. "And if that's not enough, they know we've got time warp. They'll be back; either for our technology or for us, they *will* be back."

"Comforting thought," Burnstone rasped.

Chapter Twenty:
Castaway

Lieutenant Myers leaned back into the soft polylimbicite fibers of his desk chair, fingers intertwined behind his head. The weave of the black mesh upholstery contracted and expanded in different areas to accommodate the weight and body structure of its occupant; standard issue in Space Corps' operations center, but a luxury a lieutenant could never afford to experience away from the office. The events of the past twenty-four hours were the kind of stuff a comm officer lived for, but he welcomed a little well-deserved down time.

A staccato blip sounded from the panel, jolting him out of his reverie. He tapped in several sequences and the zoomed the imaging map out until a bright orange dot flashed on the screen, the source of the signal.

"What the hell?"

Myers reconfirmed the message, then called his superior officer.

"Lieutenant," Kolanski's face appeared on the comm, "thought you'd have had enough of me for a while."

"Yes, sir…I mean…no, sir…I mean…"

Kolanski broke into a smile. "What've you got for me, son?"

"Well, sir, I'm not sure exactly. I'm getting an SOS. Old Naval signature coming in on the aliens' frequency."

Kolanski's brow furrowed. "Where's it coming from."

"Somewhere in the Bahamas. About fifty miles offshore from Paradise Island."

"Upload the exact coordinates."

"Yes, sir."

*

Kolanski hailed the general as soon as he finished reviewing the data.

"Navy? How'd the water boys get on our secure channel?" Burnstone barked.

"A better question," Kolanski answered, "is who is using a fifty year old transmitter with an outdated emergency beacon."

"Get me some answers."

"On it, sir. I've dispatched a rescue ship from Kennedy Air Field. They should be on site in a few minutes."

"Let me know when you've got something."

The line went dead before Ski could respond.

*

"I've got a visual, sir."

The feed was coming into Ski's desk real-time from the craft hovering over the Atlantic. A small capsule bobbed in the water with no frame of reference to gauge its size.

"Can you dock with it?" he asked the pilot.

"Looks like we can bring the whole thing into our cargo hold, sir. Can't be more than a couple meters long."

"Do it. And keep this feed live. I want to know what's in there before you open the hatch. Get isolation gear on before you touch that thing."

"Isolation gear?"

"Got a problem with your comm, Captain?"

"No, sir." He turned and shouted over his shoulder. "Get into gear."

The ship swooped into position within a few seconds and the grappling arms clamped onto the capsule to bring it aboard. Two men in yellow isolation suits approached cautiously. It was rare to be ordered into gear for an open water rescue.

Video feed from the visor of the ranking officer and from a camera monitoring the room was being sent simultaneously to his captain as well as to Omnicenter, where Kolanski watched events unfold on his desktop monitor. The rescue officer turned toward the capsule. He tried to wipe the fog from a window in the forward section without success; condensation was built up on the inside. He listened and felt for motion, then looked back toward the overhead camera and shook his head.

"Go ahead and open it, Lieutenant," came the orders from the shuttle's captain.

As the hatch was unsealed, Kolanski could clearly see the face of a middle aged woman with long sandy blonde hair, lying still in the cramped capsule.

"Is she alive?"

One of the men in the yellow suits bent closer. "Respirations are shallow and irregular." He waved a scanner over her. "Pulse 113."

He placed an oxygen mask over her face. "I think it's best to leave her in here until we're back. I'll get some D5 half normal saline running to hydrate her up."

The members of the crew were all trained paramedics, but their main goal was to stabilize her until they had access to a full service med facility.

"Can she make it back to Omnicenter?" Ski asked.

Kennedy would be quicker, but…" He checked her vitals again. "Yeah, she can hold on."

"Good," Kolanski said. Get her back here pronto."

"Right," the captain answered.

"Oh," Kolanski broke back in, "and can you get an ID scan?"

"Sure thing," the yellow man said. He propped open her right eye and scanned the retina. "Got that, Cap?"

The captain checked his monitor. "Computer's running it now."

"What's taking so long?" It was rare for a retinal scan to take more than a few seconds for any human in the registry.

"Beats me." The captain checked the scan image. "Looks like a clean scan…wait, it's coming up now." There was an interminable pause, then: "I'll be damned."

"What've you got?" Kolanski asked.

"You're not going to believe this one, sir."

"Try me."

"Positive ID. Samantha Jane Callahan. Born February 6, 2460, deceased June 23, 2483."

The yellow man had been listening in. "Looks pretty good for a woman who's been dead twenty years."

The captain skimmed over the data. "Seems she disappeared in the Bermuda Triangle back in 2483 along with her folks. Went out on a private boat and never came back."

"Next of kin?" Kolasnki asked.

"Just a brother…damn," he muttered.

"What is it, captain?" Kolanski had the information up on his own monitor now, but hadn't read through it all yet.

"What are the odds? The poor SOB just died yesterday. Fellow named Rhoury Jasper Callahan. Annapolis grad."

Kolanski scanned down and cross-referenced the bio on Rhoury Callahan. "Son of a bitch."

*

Within an hour of being brought into Omnicenter, Samantha Callahan's condition had stabilized. Steven Kolanski knocked politely on the door of her sick bay room.

"Come in."

He poked his head in and saw her gazing longingly up through the one window high on the wall across from the door. "How ya feeling?"

She turned to him, eyes glistening with tears. "I haven't seen a cloud in twenty years," she said softly.

Kolanski looked to the floor in silence to escape the pain of her tears, but the force of her serene smile eventually drew his gaze. Her deep blue eyes showed a strength that was thinly veiled by the moisture covering them.

"Hard to believe, isn't it?" She looked back to the small window and shook her head to a methodically slow cadence. "Twenty years…"

Kolanksi took off his hat and held it with both hands. "You up to answering a few questions?"

Sam nodded. "I was only in that pod an hour or so, and slept through most of it. I'm fine, really. In fact, I feel better than I have in a very long time."

"So, mind telling me what you were doing floating around in an escape pod from a sub that sank over a half century ago?"

"God, was it that old?"

"Fraid so."

She laughed. "Good thing I didn't know that when I climbed in."

She motioned to a chair at her bedside, and Kolanski pulled it up a little closer so they could face each other, then sat.

"So what *do* you know?"

"More than you can imagine."

"My imagination's been stretched pretty far lately."

"If I start talking about little green men are you going to lock me away?"

Kolanksi sighed. "The Silesians?"

Samantha looked at him wide eyed. "But…how do you know…"

"Let's just say I've had the displeasure."

"They're not *all* bad," Samantha said, looking down at the sheets folded across her body. "I'd be dead if it wasn't for one of them."

"Maybe you should start at the beginning, Miss Callahan."

She wiped a stray tear from the side of her eye. "Sam."

Kolasnki smiled. "Whenever you're ready, Sam."

She closed her eyes and let the memories of the last two decades wash over her, then began. At first the words came out as if she was narrating a dream, but as they continued to flow, the emotional barriers built up over twenty years began to crumble. She told him about how she had been captured, about the *Majesty* and all the people she had met, about all those she had watched die. But it was still the loss of her parents that hurt the most. Time had done little to dull the pain that showed in Sam's face.

Kolanski swallowed back the lump in his throat. "You OK?"

She shook her head as tears forced their way through tightly shut eyes. "But I will be."

"We can finish this tomorrow."

Steven Kolanski walked away with more questions than answers.

As the door shut, Sam pulled the diary out of her pocket and cradled it in both hands, then pressed it against her chest and closed her eyes.

Chapter Twenty-One:
The Escape

Kolanski was anxious to get back to Samantha Callahan to hear the rest of her story, but he'd promise to meet Danny and Jennifer for breakfast. He saw them sitting when he arrived at the commissary, and pulled up a chair.

"You're not going to believe who I found."

Danny raised an eyebrow. "Good morning to you, too."

"Oh…uh, sorry. I just haven't been able to stop thinking about her."

"Oohh." Jennifer smiled and leaned in, elbows on the table. "Give us all the juicy details."

"What?" Kolanski tilted his head. "Oh. Oh, no. It's nothing like that. I found Callahan's sister."

"Who's sister?" Stryker asked.

"Callahan. That nut case who blew up the colony."

"So what's she got to do with anything?"

"Well, it was her disappearance in the Bermuda Triangle twenty years ago that set him off. That's when he started looking for aliens in the ocean."

"Some nut case, huh?" Danny said. "So where did you find the body?"

"What body?"

Danny glared. "The sister?"

"Oh, no no no. You got me all wrong. She's *alive*. We found her in an escape pod floating out near the Bahamas yesterday…alive and well."

"So where's she been for twenty years and why did she show up right after her brother blew himself up?"

"She doesn't know about that yet."

"Hmmph. I guess you're the lucky one that gets to tell her, huh?"

Ski let out a huff and shook his head. "But as to where she's been, well that's where it really gets interesting. It seems the Silesians had more than one colony."

"So her crazy brother was right after all."

"Apparently."

"How *many* other colonies?"

"I don't know. She was really wiped out when we found her. I'm heading over to talk to her as soon as we finish up here."

"Can we tag along?" Jennifer asked.

Ski shook his head. "She's pretty fragile right now; I don't want to spook her. How about I fill you in after we talk?"

"We'll be prepping the Stargazer," Danny said. "Give us a buzz when you're done."

Kolanski stood and hurried off to meet Sam.

*

Sam was sitting at the edge of her bed in a standard issue green Space Corps hospital gown savoring her breakfast when Kolanski arrived.

"God," she mumbled through a mouthful of scrambled eggs, "I forgot how good these are."

Ski motioned to the chair across from where she sat. "May I?"

She nodded and he sat, hat in hand.

She shoveled in another fork full of eggs, then took a swig of coffee.

"Take your time," he said with a grin.

She waved a hand at him and swallowed. "Sorry," she sputtered, then washed down the remainder of her eggs with another gulp from the steaming mug.

"No problem. What'd they feed you down there anyway?"

"Rations from downed vessels when they had them, various seafood concoctions most other times. Haven't had a cup of coffee with fresh cream in ages."

He took a deep breath. "I think I'd miss that the most."

She held the mug between her hands and floated on the aroma for a very long moment, then reluctantly put it on the tray. "It was a very strange couple of decades down there."

"Did they treat you OK?"

"Oh, *God* yes," she said without hesitation. "Like honored guests, in their own bizarre way. They knew very little about humans and didn't seem too anxious to find out. It was more like they didn't want us around, but they were afraid to *not* be polite. Something about offending their sense of decency. Mostly, they ignored us."

"Then why keep you alive? I know that sounds rough, but if they didn't need you, why go to all that effort to keep you alive?"

She shrugged. "Same reason we would, I guess. Because it's the humane thing to do."

Sam took a long sip of coffee and closed her eyes. When she reopened them, it was as if she'd just looked back into the past.

"At first, it was the other survivors that filled me in. But once I got the radio working and made contact, that's when I really started to learn."

"You actually communicated with them?"

Sam nodded. "Like I said yesterday, I couldn't raise anyone topside, but I was determined to try and establish a link with our captors. I kept trying various frequencies, and then one day something came back. It was a bunch of clicks and squeals. At first, I thought the radio was fried, but then I realized it wasn't just random noise. So I tried transmitting a single word: *hello*. After a few seconds, this weird sound came back. I sent the same thing again; got the same reply. We played that game for a while until about the tenth time when a high pitched hello sounded back at me. I almost fell out of my chair. The alien on the other end was learning English.

"It took almost three years of tedium. I spent just about every waking hour in that room, and eventually he learned enough English that we could communicate. That's when I started to find out what had been happening."

"Amazing." Kolanski tapped his hat against his free hand. "But if they learned English, then why didn't the others use it when we talked to them?"

"You *talked* to them? The *others*?"

"Uh…yeah," Ski stammered. "It's kind of a long story."

"I've got nothing but time, Colonel." She looked pleadingly into his eyes.

Ski hesitated briefly, then shrugged. "Hell, I guess if anybody deserves to know, you do. I'll tell you what I can when we're done here."

"Fair enough," Sam said, then shook her head slowly. "Wow. I didn't even know they still existed – the *others*, that is. Nyah – that's the one I made contact with – he told me his group had separated from the others centuries ago. Shortly after the Silesians first arrived on Earth there was a disagreement amongst the crew. Most wanted to stay in hiding until a rescue ship came. But some of them weren't so sure help would ever get here. They decided to make their way to shallower water where they could observe what was going on with human evolution, know what they were up against and whether there was ever a chance they could safely co-exist with humans. They never had contact with the original colony again."

"Didn't they ever go back to look for them?"

"They were afraid to venture that far away. They made a life for themselves down there.

"Nyah confirmed what we all suspected, that they periodically downed air and sea vessels directly over their position to keep tabs on how technology was changing; the humans in those ships were simply an annoyance they had to deal with. They didn't want to kill anybody, but they couldn't risk giving away their position either.

"They devised some sort of environmental bubble to encase whatever they wanted to bring down, and everything inside that bubble, atmosphere and people included, were pulled to the bottom of the sea. They soon realized that humans couldn't survive like that for very long; they needed air, food, a place to exercise; they needed companionship and challenges to occupy their minds. They needed a much larger ship.

"When the *Majesty* was brought down, the environmental bubble became unstable; it wasn't designed for something of that scale. There were rapid pressure fluctuations as they fought to maintain the force field. The ship made it down with little damage but no one on board survived. The Silesians were overcome with guilt and determined to improve the process to protect human life; they consider themselves a pacifistic race."

Ski shook his head.

"What?"

"Nothing. Go on."

Sam frowned. "I really think I deserve a little more honesty, Colonel."

"And you'll get it, Sam. But I need to know what you know first. The sooner we know what we're dealing with, the better. I promise I'll give you the full story when we're done…if that's what you really want."

"That's what I want."

"It'll take a commitment you may not want to make, a commitment to the Corps."

Sam bit back her lip. "I'm not sure I can make that promise, but I deserve to know."

"You'll know everything that's not classified; everything else if you're on the inside."

She understood the military mentality and continued with a nod.

"They treated us well, but thought we were too primitive to warrant communicating with. Until Nyah. He wanted to learn what makes us tick, what the chances were that humanity might accept the Silesians in peace. I had to tell him his chances weren't good. It sealed my fate, but it was the truth."

Ski shifted back in the chair and crossed his legs. "Then how did you get away?"

"The day you found me there was a lot of commotion. We'd never seen so much action on the far side of the dome. They must have sensed it before we did. The tremors started softly, but kept increasing in frequency and intensity. The Silesians were in a frenzy before we noticed the integrity of the dome starting to fail. I ran to the radio room to contact Nyah and he was already on the other end trying to raise me. He instructed me to go to the second bubble, the one where they were studying debris from various ships. That dome also had a breathable atmosphere; they tried to keep it as close as possible to surface conditions to preserve the confiscated technology. Anyhow, when I got there, Nyah had opened a portal to let me into the other dome. One of the robotic arms guided me to the escape pod. I climbed in just before the dome collapsed. That's the last thing I remember before you found me."

"What about the others?"

Sam shook her head and held back the tears. "There was no time to warn them. And even if I could have, there was no place for them to hide."

She sobbed and Kolanski looked toward the ray of light slipping in through the small window above.

Her voice was weak. "God, I feel so guilty."

"There's nothing you could have done. You said so yourself."

"But I should have been there with them."

"To what end? Give up your life for a few seconds of comfort that would most likely have been lost in the panic? No, Sam. They'd have wanted you to get out and tell their story. They'd have been furious with you if you hadn't taken advantage of that opportunity. Through you, what they endured will live on."

Sam dabbed her nose with a napkin and smiled. "Thanks."

He acknowledged her and stood. "I'll give you a little time."

"Wait." She stopped him mid turn. "I want to know. I *need* to know what happened up here."

He stood silently, looking into her eyes.

"And I need to find my brother."

Chapter Twenty-Two:
Suspicions

Danny and Jennifer were sitting and waiting at the same table they'd had breakfast at when Kolanski entered the commissary.

Danny waved him over. "You look like you've been hit by a truck."

"She took it pretty hard."

"Did you expect any different?" Jennifer asked.

He shook his head. "That didn't make it any easier."

"So what'd you find out?"

Ski recounted her story in as much detail as he could muster.

"Wow," Jennifer huffed. "Twenty years? That's incredible."

Danny leaned forward, elbows propped on the table and fingers intertwined. "So if those SOB's could speak English, why'd they make us squeal like pigs to get their attention?"

"From what I can gather, that colony lived in isolation for centuries. They probably hadn't communicated with the Atlantic colony or the mother ship."

"And they just happened to get wiped out by a quake the same day all that crap went down with the others?"

Jennifer shook her head. "Not likely. The mother ship must have picked them up on scans and taken them out with some sort of weapon, wiped them out for the same reasons they wanted that other colony destroyed."

"Makes sense," Kolanski agreed. "Probably took out any other colonies that may have been here too. That's the good news. There shouldn't be any more Silesians down there."

Danny frowned. "But they're aquatic. Even if their homes were destroyed, couldn't they just swim off and live somewhere else?"

"I asked Sam that very question," Ski said. "But think about it. The aliens on the mother ship wanted all the colonists dead, and more than likely knew just how to make that happen. And even if by some chance they missed a few, the survivors would be isolated. It would be like taking one of us and depositing us in a jungle on Earth back in the Jurassic Period. How long you think you'd survive that?"

Danny took a deep breath. "So that's that."

"Still," Kolanski added, "we need to do some exploring and see what's left down there. Think Blake would want in?"

Jennifer shook her head. "He's got his hands full catching up back at Woods Hole, then he and Margo are going to help me out back at the Shakespeare Center. I'm not going to let you steal them away from me."

"The android shop? What're a couple of marine biologists going to do there?"

"We've obviously got a lot to learn about how to function under water. Hopefully we can develop some adaptations that can help us in case the Silesians show again some day."

"I thought you said the threat of," he glanced around, "you know…will keep them away."

"One can only hope. But let's face it, that technology may prove to be more of a lure than a threat. We need to be ready."

*

Jennifer and Danny strolled down the corridors of Space Corps Command heading for the landing bay to prepare for the trip back to Kennedy Prime.

As they rounded the corner, Professor Quigley was leaning against a wall, waiting. "I heard you two were heading out today. Glad I caught you." He looked at Jennifer. "Can I steal you away for a minute?"

She reached over and gave Danny's hand a squeeze. "Go on. I'll meet you aboard."

Danny nodded. "See you, Professor," he said with a wave as he turned to walk away.

"Oh, Stryker," Quigley said.

Danny turned.

"Hell of a job out there."

"Yeah," Danny said with a smile, "it was, wasn't it." He turned and walked away with a lilt in his step.

Jennifer smiled as she watched Danny walk off.

"That was a nice thing to say, Q," she said softly.

"Ah, those things slip out sometimes," Quigley grinned.

She swatted his arm playfully.

The characteristic joviality faded from his face. "So how'd you do it, Jen?"

She sighed deeply. "I'm really tired, Q. How about we go over the schematics tomorrow?"

"Not the photonic feedback," he said with a slight shake of the head. "I know you couldn't have done *that*."

"*Excuse* me?" Jennifer straightened her back and glared.

Quigley let out a laugh. "Oh, come on. I mean *Blake*," he said. "How did you do *that*?"

"Blake?" she said quizzically.

"He's remarkable."

"Hey, I've only got eyes for Danny."

"Which is why Blake looks like his little brother," Quigley said. "It's amazing. He's so…*human*."

Jennifer glanced around nervously.

"Ah, don't worry," he said. "Your secret's safe with me."

"You do entertain me, Q," she said through a forced giggle, "but I'm beat." She dismissed him with a wave of the hand and started down the hall. After a few steps, her pace slowed to a halt and she turned. Her mouth opened as if to speak, but she simply shook her head and walked away.

Quigley stood there, leaning against the wall with his arms crossed, smiling after her.

Even the things that go *Bump* in the night
will learn that you <u>DON'T</u> mess with...
Terrorbelle.

"Thomas certainly brings the goods to the table when it comes to writing urban fiction...I promise, you will love... Terrorbelle: Fairy With a Gun. Who doesn't love a well-stacked, ass-kicking, gun-toting, woman with bullet-proof, razor-sharp wings that investigates all manner of supernatural spookiness? I know I do, and Thomas's humor shows through in every tale. Jim Butcher and Laurell K Hamilton have nothing on Thomas." The Raven's Barrow

From The Murphy's Lore Universe Of
PATRICK THOMAS

www. padwolf.com & www.terrorbelle.com

The shout has echoed throughout history, "Barbarians at the gate!" Words that strike terror in the hearts of civilized peoples everywhere. If we have learned anything from our past, it is that history repeats itself. So on a grim day in the future when less civilized aliens attack us will we cry, "BARBARIANS AT THE JUMPGATE!"

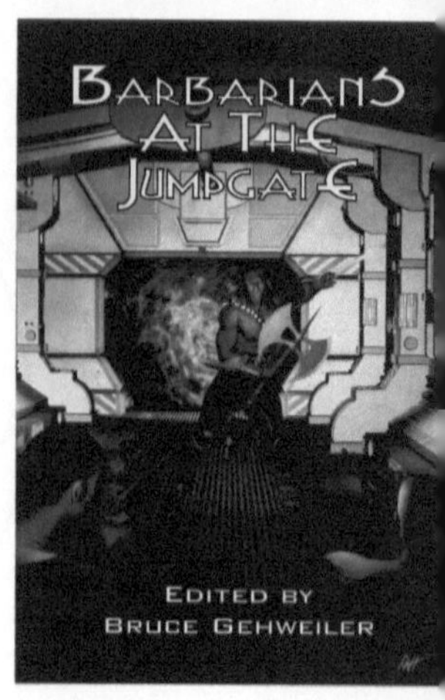

Award winning author and editor Bruce Gehweiler has gathered together for the first time fifteen fresh tales of science fiction and fantasy adventure that hearken back to the golden age of science fiction. Join C.J. Henderson, Patrick Thomas, Danielle Ackley-McPhail, John Sunseri, Robert E. Waters, James Chambers, Bernie Mojzes, James Daniel Ross, R. Allen Leider, Neal Levin, Lawrence Barker, and Darren W. Pearce on a wild ride through towering imaginations and an uncertain future as great civilizations fight against hordes of Barbarians... in the future!

Hidden from the eyes of mankind they lurk in the shadows. In remote parts of our planet they survive the passage of time. Brave men and women seek out these unknown creatures in a search for truth that is muddled in legends and folklore-scoffed at by modern science. These are the tales of cryptozoology, the study of hidden and unknown animals.

CRYPTO-CRITTERS
VOLUMES 1 & 2

Got Blood? We do and as everyone knows new blood is simply the best. With these pages we have wonder and fangs aplenty including a cyborg vampire in space, steampunk vamps, a werewolf PI, a vampire escalator, blood suckers in love, a study in orthodox vampirism, the undead at war and of course a cannabilistically incestuous vampire penguin from Coney Island. And that's just the begining.

Join New York Times Best Selling Author and multiple Bram Stoker award winner Jonathan Maberry, Bram Stoker Winner Linda Addison, fantasy legends C.J. Henderson and Rowena Morrill, award winners Danielle Ackley-McPhail and Brad Aiken, alongside some of the best writers in the business - James Chambers, William H. Horner III, Neal Levin, Jeff Lyman, Bernie Mojzes, Terri Osborne, K.T. Pinto, Diane Raetz, T.L. Randleman, Hildy Silverman, John Sunseri and Patrick Thomas - as they bring you tales of vampires you never dreamed existed and others that will forever haunt your nightmares.

www.ingramcontent.com/pod-product-compliance
Lightning Source LLC
Chambersburg PA
CBHW061925220726
48287CB00018B/921